Pride, Prejudice and the Perfect Match

MARILYN BRANT

WHITE SOUP PRESS

White Soup Press
First CreateSpace Edition

ISBN-10: 1-4825-7446-2
ISBN-13: 978-1-4825-7446-3

DEDICATION

For Austen lovers everywhere and in special celebration of the 200th anniversary of PRIDE AND PREJUDICE, one of the world's greatest literary masterpieces.
Thank you, Jane!

OTHER BOOKS BY MARILYN BRANT:

CONTENTS

PRAISE FOR MARILYN BRANT'S NOVELS

Pride, Prejudice and the Perfect Match

"Brant couldn't have done a better job at pulling me into the story and keeping me hooked until the end... I liked this book so much that I delayed watching the Season 3 premiere of Downton Abbey!! (This is a huge deal.)"
~Austenprose

"Heartwarming, tender and sweet—Pride, Prejudice and the Perfect Match is a lovely tribute to Jane Austen and her masterpiece." ~Austenesque Reviews

According to Jane

"A charming book." ~Family Circle

"Fresh, original, and lots of fun." ~Barnes & Noble Review

"Brant infuses her sweetly romantic and delightfully clever tale with just the right dash of Austen-esque wit."
~Chicago Tribune

"Marilyn Brant's debut novel is proof that Jane Austen never goes out of style. This is a warm, witty and charmingly original story..." ~#1 New York Times Bestselling Author Susan Wiggs

A Summer in Europe

"Brant's newest...distinguishes itself with a charismatic leading man and a very funny supporting cast, especially the wonderful elderly characters with their resonant message about living life to the fullest." ~Publishers Weekly

"Marilyn Brant's A Summer in Europe is a wonderful tale that captivates readers as Gwen, transformed by her surroundings, undergoes a change of heart about life...and love." ~Doubleday Book Club

"Oh, this book is like sitting in the sun in the middle of a Roman piazza while eating a big scoop of gelato. It's lovely and something to be savored... Sigh, this was so good; like a vacation in a book." ~A Bookish Affair

On Any Given Sundae

"You'll want to read it for the humor and great characters and a plot that's sure to leave you smiling." ~Romantic Times Book Reviews

"This is truly a root-for-the-underdog, feel-good story and a joy to read." ~Chicklit Club

"I absolutely positively ADORED this book." ~Romancing the Book

ACKNOWLEDGMENTS

With heartfelt thanks
to my friends and family,
who have so consistently supported
me and my writing.
You've been relentlessly encouraging
on challenging days and
joyously willing to share in the celebration
on happy ones.
And I know
I couldn't have made a career
out of being a novelist
without you!

CHAPTER ONE

Beth Ann Bennet typed "male" in the box that indicated which gender she was seeking. Her best friend and fellow classmate, Jane Henderson, leaned over her shoulder and studied the university library's computer screen in the afternoon sunlight. The cursor blinked, and Beth's level of nausea rose with each flash.

"So far, so good," her friend declared.

Beth seriously doubted it.

"This has to be illegal, or maybe just immoral." She bit down on her lip again, the one she'd chewed until it'd turned raw and achy. "Somehow I doubt Professor O'Reilly had this method in mind when he told us to gather sociological data."

Jane tilted her auburn head and gave Beth that familiar when-are-you-gonna-get-with-the-program look. She exhaled melodramatically. "For goodness sake, Beth Ann, this is *research*. It's not like you're going to get emotionally invested or anything. Heaven knows, you'll drop the dimwit like a dead goldfish before he has a chance to ask any questions. Find an appropriate case study, get the info and get out. Kids' stuff."

"For you, maybe," Beth said, wondering for the seven hundredth time why she'd let herself get talked into this. "You've playacted with your identity since you were— what, a toddler? I haven't."

Jane flashed a grin of discernible pride, which was combined in equal measure with deviousness. Beth's spirits sank a notch lower. Why couldn't she be more like her best friend? Jane was light years ahead of her in the deceit department.

"C'mon," Jane said. "Next question."

"Okay. Between the ages of…?"

"Well, you're twenty-six, but you'll be playing it younger of course." Jane squinted at the screen. "Go for men in the twenty-five to thirty-five range."

"Fine." Beth typed in the information. "Located within…?"

"No further than a twenty-mile radius of your Chicago ZIP code."

She keyed that in also, her pulse picking up speed.

"Now, check the 'photos only' box and click on GO. I want to see if the rumors are true."

"You know as well as I do that this is a scam. I mean, seriously. *Lady Catherine's Love Match Website—Where You're Destined To Find Your Perfect Mate?*" Beth forced a laugh. "We may succeed in proving gender-role stereotypes are alive and well in the New Millennium, but there's no way we'll snag a guy who'll prove true love can be found through an e-search."

Jane smirked then aimed an index finger at the screen. "Scroll down and let's get a peek at your—holy shmoly— *fifty-four* potential Love Matches. Not that I'm dying to be a bridesmaid or anything but—"

Beth elbowed her.

"Ouch!"

"Shhh. We're in a library."

Jane rolled her eyes in response.

Beth closed hers before threading her fingers through her tangled mop of light-brown hair. She felt the split ends snap.

She groaned and wished she could afford a decent haircut. But no. March meant paying off the final installment of her tuition bill and what she made at work could only stretch so far. Plus, there were necessities like bread and peanut butter, staple items for a mom with a six-year-old. If everything went as she planned, maybe by June she could justify an appointment.

She opened her eyes and glared at the listing of eligible men, reminding herself that she *had* to choose one. They swam through her range of vision while the lyrics to "Looking for Love in All the Wrong Places" flooded her brain. She tried to block out the tune and focus on the faces of her research subjects. Who'd make the best candidate?

Jane, quick study that she was, had zeroed in on someone already. "Oh, Beth. Just look at Number 16. Blue-eyed. Beefy. And he likes children."

Beefy was right. He had muscles the size of overgrown cantaloupes. And, oh, he preferred blondes.

"My soul mate for sure." She ignored Jane's protests and scrolled further down the screen. She had one shot at this and refused to mess it up. "Number 23 has some potential, though. He claims to be athletic. And 'spiritual.' Into fast cars. Watches 'Must-See TV.' And he's seeking someone in the skinny to slim range. Sounds like an ideally stereotypical guy."

She kept reading.

Whoa.

"Except he's proud of his Streisand CD collection, his Chia Pet and his Virgo perfectionism. These things could throw off the hypothesis." Beth sighed.

Jane read the name. "Reverend Ezekiel Collins is not typical enough for you?"

"Maybe not."

"Moving on then."

"What do you think of Number 37?" Beth said.

Jane wrinkled her upturned nose.

"Yeah. Me neither," she conceded, "but I'm running out of options."

Then she saw him.

She centered his profile on the screen. Read the bio. Reread it while Jane's giggles bubbled around her. Heaven help her, but Number 49 was The One.

"So, it'll be 'Will Darcy' then, eh?" Jane said. "Likes women of every hair color. Very open-minded of him."

"It's all there," she whispered, marveling at the image of the man before her. "The sports interest. The standard descriptive lines. A professed 'love of the outdoors' and other oh-so-masculine pursuits."

"You're right. He likes camping. Yuck."

"No mention of cooking together, dancing 'til dawn or seeing sappy chick-flicks, like some of these other guys. At least we can't question his honesty. No unusual club affiliations. And he even admits to having strong professional ambitions, although he doesn't elaborate."

"Definitely falls into an acceptable salary range," Jane agreed, pointing to the numbers listed in the right-hand column.

"And just take a peek at what he's looking for. Someone 'attractive, college-educated, height/weight proportionate'—meaning almost anorexic." Beth raised her eyebrows. "Someone 'twenty-one to twenty-five who likes children but has no dependents.' They all want a woman who's young and unencumbered. I swear, this guy sounds like every blind date I've had in the past five years."

Her friend gave her a scrutinizing once-over. "You're slim, pretty, you've got great bone structure and those huge brown eyes, and you could pass for twenty-two without a second thought."

Beth shrugged. So what if she looked young? One's age wasn't something a person could hide forever. "Maybe," she said. "And I'm almost, finally, college-educated. But there's still that little question of dependents..."

"He doesn't need to know about Charlie or your real occupation or even your real name, Beth. Use an alias. Maybe that combination of your parents' names—Charlotte and Lucas—that you pretended was your penname when you were ten."

Jane tapped her chin. "Besides, you might as well try for someone you think is kind of cute. If all goes well, you'll have to spend hours analyzing the guy. Maybe even a few studying him in person—without getting too close of course," she warned. "It's okay to have a little fun with your online profile."

Beth shuddered. The things she had to endure in the name of science. Well, social science.

But perhaps Jane was right. If she had to do this final Sociology 369 "Gender and Society" project, and if she was in the quarter of the class that had to use the Internet as her main research tool, she might as well choose a subject who was at least tall, dark-haired and gorgeous. Nothing stereotypical about her own mate selection, of course, she thought. The irony of it brought the day's first grin to her lips.

She lifted her fingers to the keyboard and clicked on the REPLY button to send Number 49 an email:

Hello, Will. I'm a twenty-two-year-old child psychology major, Beth began. She glanced back at her friend.

"Yeah, that's perfect," Jane said. "Use my major. It'll explain your knowledge of children without giving anything away. I can fill you in on subject details later."

Beth nodded. *I love the outdoors and particularly enjoy playing softball,* she typed, and then grimaced at the blatant lies. The guilt was already eating at her, but she had to think of her son. Nothing could get in the way of her providing for Charlie. She continued, *I'm hoping we might correspond and get to know one another better. My name is Charlotte Lucas and you can email me at…*

***

In the Regents General Hospital cafeteria a few weeks later, Dr. William Darcy gulped his last swallow of the Mocha-Cappuccino De-latte Delight he'd gotten at the gourmet coffee shop nearby. Then he glared at his cousin. "No, I don't want to bet a hundred bucks on whether or not you can catch a fish stick between your teeth."

Bingley McNamara grinned, crossed his long legs at the ankles and propped them up on the metal chair to Will's left. "Face it, Cuz. You're intimidated by my varied and remarkable skills." He tossed his last greasy fish stick in the air and caught it neatly between his incisors. He chomped down. "I'd have won," he said around a mouthful of deep-fried pseudo-fish. "My talent frightens you."

"The only thing about you that frightens me is your insatiable gambling habit." Will leveled his most disapproving stare at the guy but, as usual, his cousin ignored him.

"Aw, c'mon. Everyone makes a wager now and then."

"Only if 'now and then' means every fifteen minutes." Will scanned his watch. "Go. Get out of here. Although this may be a foreign concept to you, I've actually got a job."

"I've got a job," Bingley said, sounding indignant. "It's just a little less, oh, how should I put it? Obvious."

"Overseeing your trust fund is not a bona fide career. It's a sick obsession. Although how it manages to grow profits, despite your wagering addiction, is a mystery."

"Jealous?"

"No."

Bingley snorted, guzzled his short Colombian espresso then sent Will a semi-serious look. "Listen up. Did you give any more thought to my proposition last month? Any bites online?"

Will turned his back on his favorite and only cousin, who—at present—he wanted to strangle to within a millimeter of the rich party boy's life. He pitched the remains of their lunch in the trash then loosened his tie.

"And what if I have?" Will said finally, knowing he'd regret even considering Bingley's latest ludicrous bet. But, dammit, he needed the help and he needed it now. "Are you prepared to follow through if I can get the lady to materialize?"

"Not just any lady," Bingley reminded him. "A girlfriend who could take an active role in your precious clinic." He sniffed. "That'll give you a shot at wanting to be with her long term. I expect a five-date minimum, and I need to meet her before the second Sunday in May."

"Listen, Bingley—"

"I know you don't believe me, but I'm looking out for your best interests here, Cuz. Before I plunk my money into some do-good operation, I want proof that you've finally gotten a life outside of this, this...morgue." He waved the arm with the Rolex attached to it in a wild loopy arc. "Evidence that you've scored a little balance in your daily life—among other things." He waggled his brows suggestively.

Will marveled at how a guy who resembled him physically could act with all the subtlety of a Saturday-morning cartoon character.

"So keep the movie-ticket stubs from your dates," Bingley said. "Learn how to use the camera app on your phone, or even grab your old Polaroid, and snap some pretty pictures of the two of you. Save her emails and make sure she shows up happy and talkative by my birthday. It's on Mother's Day, this year." He tilted his head as if in deep contemplation. "Whoever this chick is, I wanna see her hanging on your arm with lovely-dovey eyes only for you."

Will thought of the one woman he wanted, no, *needed* to win this wager with Bingley. Charlotte Lucas. If only she could be as amazing in person as she seemed online. A youthful but professional twenty-two-year-old future child psychologist. Bright, humorous and a sports enthusiast with a warm heart. Someone who'd fit in perfectly at the clinic, if he'd gauged her right. And someone he could tolerate for five dates outside of it.

She'd described herself as being five-foot-six with light-brown hair and brown eyes, but she held the advantage. She'd seen him—a scanned picture anyway—but he had yet to see her. Maybe, just maybe, after three weeks of cautious emailing, that'd change tomorrow. The clinic's funding depended on it.

Still, this was a hell of a way to make a few million bucks.

"I've got to go," he said. "My rounds start in a few

minutes. Talk to you next week."

"Catch you later," his cousin said. "Don't be a stranger."

"They don't come any stranger than you," Will muttered, their standard childhood reply.

"I heard that." Bingley smirked, his fingers scoring his thick brown hair, his lean legs sauntering on his way through the sliding doors.

Will sighed and took to the stairs. The guy never changed. There was always some weird bet, some eccentric agenda in Bingley's quest to "feel needed" or whatever. But this time the ends might justify the means.

Will tucked the flap of his shirt into the dress slacks he'd worn for the administrative meeting today and readjusted his tie with a scowl. He missed his scrubs but formalities had to be observed with the hospital board.

"Hey, Dr. Darcy," a ninety-year-old patient called from her bed on the second-floor east wing. "You my doctor today?"

"Wish I was, sweetheart," he said, winking and making the elderly lady blush. "None of the patients on my roster could hold a candle to your good looks."

"Oh, how you do go on!" She looked away, her head and hands shaking, feigning disbelief, but he could see teeth. She was grinning big.

Parkinson's. Stage Two. He struggled to close his mind to it and move down the hall. The pain of dealing with deteriorating elderly patients would chew him up if he dwelled there. Even though the low-income moms he liked to work with were often in dire straits, it was still less agonizing to watch than the suffering of the elderly.

He slid into an empty room and flipped on the computer. He had huge plans for his clinic. He just needed to get the hospital's final stamp of approval, which he could get if he could secure the rest of the cash.

The board had said so.

This morning.

To get the cash, though, he'd have to get Bingley onboard. To get Bingley onboard, he'd have to get Charlotte Lucas.

Immediately.

He scanned his list of unread email messages, but didn't see anything life-threatening in the subject lines. Clicking on Charlotte's email address, he typed what he hoped would be a hard-to-resist invitation.

Will proofed it for errors, took a deep breath and clicked SEND.

***

"With Mimi leaving us, we've got maybe a month's leeway before someone else has to step in." Dan Noelen, Beth's fieldwork sponsor and part-time boss at Chicago Social Services, brushed a tuft of graying hair off his high forehead and grimaced. "Robby's able to cover about half the families. Abby said she could take on eight or nine others, but there are a couple of elderly folks near Regents General Hospital who'll need looking in on by a social worker. Think you can handle it, Beth?"

"Absolutely," she said, trying to project professionalism, responsibility and a hard-to-miss level of eagerness. "Just show me what needs to be done."

Dan motioned her into his office. He shut the door. "Listen, I trust you. I know you can pick up the slack on these older clients." He handed her two thick manila file folders labeled with the names Anne Marie Dermott and Lynn Hammond.

"If you're interested in interviewing for Mimi's position, I'm open to the idea. You've done an excellent job with your field experience here, and your extra work as a part-time assistant is outstanding. Thing is, though, even for entry-level social work, the degree is essential." He rested a paternal hand on her shoulder. "No incompletes. No failed classes. Nothing marring your academic record. You graduate next month, right?"

"Right. Third weekend in May."

"When you've got the diploma in your hands, let me know pronto. I can run the interview and make the recommendation, but I still have to submit your paperwork officially to the board of directors. And for this position, it's all got to be in before June first."

"Thanks, Dan. There won't be any problems. I just have one last sociology class to finish and, of course, my field instruction here."

He smiled at her. "Good. We need people like you in this agency, kid. Now, get to work."

She left his office and collapsed at her makeshift desk, smiling with glee and goodwill toward the entire planet. Another month or so and she'd have a real desk with drawers, not just a glorified end table with a computer on it and a photo of her son Charlie squished off to the side. She'd be a true professional! Respected finally. Man, she could hardly wait.

Beth plunked the files down and scanned the individual care plans. Reading their reports, her heart clenched in sympathy. Getting old must be hard. Her favorite relative, Grandma Kate, used to complain so.

"The body doesn't do what it should anymore," Grandma would say, handing Beth an enormous oatmeal-raisin cookie before wiping her arthritic fingers on her apron. "And there's no one to listen to you whine after awhile. They all up and die."

Beth picked up the framed photo of her son. She ran a finger down his two-dimensional cheek, wishing she were touching the real one.

But Charlie was busy at school, no doubt plaguing his kindergarten teacher with incessant questions. He barely knew *his* grandparents—her parents, the Bennets. They lived in Arizona now, and her mother wouldn't be caught baking cookies if her golf swing depended on it.

As for the other set of grandparents, well, they tended to forget they had a grandson. Just like her ex-husband Pete Wickham, Charlie's father, forgot he had a son.

"You and me, babycakes," she whispered, admiring the straight, blond hair so unlike her own and the silken skin only a child could possess. "Things are looking up for us."

The computer gave a frantic beep, alerting her to another email. After adding "Organize Clients' Data" to the bottom of her To Do list, she turned her attention to deleting spam. Only a few noteworthy messages remained: Some requested information on hospice care. Updates from the university's social work department. An offer for ten percent off her next oil change.

The computer beeped again.

Sender: William Darcy.

She gasped, her blood pressure jumping up to a level not advised by health professionals.

She let the cursor hover over his name on the screen. *Doctor* Darcy. What would Number 49 write this time?

He'd sent her seven emails in the last few weeks, telling her of his profession and his coffee addiction. His love of baseball, hotdogs, apple pie and...Ferrari. She'd saved and printed every one. The Good Doctor had a funny online personality. He seemed so sincere.

But he also seemed very stereotypical, she reminded herself. The kind of guy who wouldn't look at her twice if he knew she were closer to thirty than to twenty, had a school-aged son, hadn't yet earned a college degree and supported herself by working part-time as a lowly social-work assistant.

She'd answered him of course—for research purposes only—her heart hammering its way out of her chest every time she hit the SEND button. If she didn't desperately need that information for her final paper, she would've acted ethically and broken it off at least five emails ago.

But she *did* need the information and, furthermore, something about this guy kept luring her back.

Curiosity got the better of her, and she clicked on his message.

Hi, Charlotte! Glad to know you're fond of hot coffee and home-baked cookies, too. (Well, not everything she told him was a lie.) *The things we have in common are piling up. What do you say we take a small step forward and try out both of the above? There's a Koffee Haus near the hospital. Their brew is strong and they make a mean chocolate-chip cookie. Any interest in meeting me there tomorrow afternoon? Let me know.*—*Will*

Meet him?

No way. Although…

She could get her answers faster in person. That might be the easiest way to simultaneously complete her research and end things with tact. He'd realize she wasn't as young as he'd expected, or remotely hip or wealthy. He'd talk to her for twenty minutes to be polite and then rush out of there. All communication would dwindle to nothing within a week or two.

Maybe…

She hit the REPLY key, staring at the blank space where her return message needed to go. She should say, *No, thank you.* She should say, *Sorry, although I've enjoyed emailing you, I'm not ready to meet in person.* She should say, *I'm on a strict diet and can't go near bakery items.* Anything.

Her fingers, however, had ideas of their own. They flew over the keyboard as if racing against logic.

Lovely plan, Will. I can be there at one p.m. tomorrow. See you then.—Charlotte

Her fingers hit the SEND button before her mind had a chance to talk them out of it.

***

The next day at dawn, Beth reviewed her stereotypes list:

1. Greater size and strength
2. Goal-oriented, often highly ambitious
3. Values the rational/logical over the emotional
4. More independent, assertive, critical & competitive
5. Fast visual-attraction reactions
6. Better at spatial/mathematical skills
7. Difficulty expressing emotions

Yep. That seemed to pretty much sum up the major male stereotypes as she knew them, omitting universal truths like men's bizarre predilection toward big tools and bigger remote-control devices.

Beth laid down her pen. She was armed and ready for today's coffee "date" and planned to find as much direct, supporting evidence as she could for each point in the few minutes she and Will would spend together. She prayed she'd be able to pull it off.

Somehow she managed to get Charlie to school, do a morning's worth of organizing at the agency and pull into the Koffee Haus parking lot right on time.

The scent of warm, roasted coffee beans enticed her nostrils even before she made it through the doorway. The singles' bar of this century had cinnamon shakers and skim milk pitchers on the counter instead of vodka jiggers and salty peanuts, but the idea was unchanged.

A pair of lanky guys leaned against the counter

waiting for their orders to be ready. Neither of them looked anything like Will's website photograph. Where was he?

A small table opened up near the door and Beth leaped for it. She slid into the chair and began casing the room. Mostly couples or small groups of friends. A dark-haired man in his early thirties sat alone with a newspaper. His back was to her so she leaned to the left to try to catch a glimpse of his face.

It could be him. Might be.

She leaned a little further but before she could see him she felt that roller-coaster dip in her stomach and lost her balance—hands swiping the floor, chair scraping awkwardly. Very smooth move.

The guy turned to stare at her. So did everyone else. She readjusted herself and tried to bury her head in her purse.

That looked like him. Close enough to the photo anyway to make her pretty sure. Darn it. There was no way he'd want to be approached by a klutz.

When she looked up, he was staring at her again. An assessing glance. Yep. The game was over before it had a chance to begin. Something about him struck her as odd, though. His email personality was so warm, so charming. This guy—well, arrogant seemed to be a better descriptor.

She wondered what he'd do now. Ditch her? She grabbed her stereotypes list from her purse, scanning it covertly in case he worked up the nerve to come over before she approached him. A glimpse at her watch told her it was already ten minutes past one. When she looked back at his table, he was gone.

She sighed. This wasn't good. Her final project was due in a few weeks, and she needed to cite concrete examples of Case Study #1's behavior, documented and dated over a period of thirty days. She didn't have time to start again with a new subject. As it was, she'd have to use all of their email correspondence in her report, and that still left her with over a week's worth of communication to obtain and record.

And nothing she had thus far was very conclusive.

She didn't want to resort to shortcuts to complete the paper, but Charlie's future was at stake here. She stood to leave.

"So, are you the woman Lady Catherine thinks I'm destined for?" a deep voice with a laugh hidden in it whispered in her ear.

She swiveled around and stared at the man behind her. He wasn't the guy with the newspaper, but he, too, looked like Will's website photo… only better. Much better.

"If so," he continued, "I'm your Perfect Match."

CHAPTER TWO

She was a knockout, pure and simple. Tanned skin, wild tufts of light-brown hair, huge dark eyes that looked both inquisitive and kind. Will took in the startled expression on Charlotte Lucas's angelic face and drew in a lungful of air. She'd literally robbed him of his breath. He had no choice but to snatch it back.

"William Darcy?"

He nodded. "Call me Will. And you must be Charlotte." She didn't answer. She just kept staring at him. "Been here long?"

"No, not really, but I—um—didn't see you come in. Actually, I thought for a minute that someone else was the person I was supposed to meet. He looked a lot like your profile picture and was sitting over there…" She pointed to a table near the back.

Bingley's spot. Will had seen him through the window and snuck in the back door to dodge him. He'd forgotten when he'd emailed her this location that it was one of his cousin's favorite haunts.

Bingley needed to meet the stunning Miss Lucas for

sure, to validate the agreement and everything, just not on this very first date. Will wanted to at least attempt to make a good initial impression, and his cousin would have made that impossible.

He tried to shrug nonchalantly. "Who knows? They say we all have a twin somewhere." He motioned for her to sit back down. "Sorry I'm a few minutes late. I got detained at the hospital."

"Oh, that's all right. I'm glad you made it. It's nice— very nice—to finally meet you. Busy morning?" She brushed a strand of untamed hair behind her ear and fiddled with her purse straps.

"Yeah." Jeez, but did she ever seem nervous. How much coffee did she drink while she was waiting? He shot a glance to the bar. "Have you had a chance to order anything?"

She shook her head and he immediately rose, feeling her eyes watching him. "Let me get you a drink. What would you like?"

"Oh, thank you. Just a small decaf." She rummaged in her purse for a few bills and some change. "Here, I've got—"

He covered her hand with his and felt the rapid pulse beneath her knuckles. "My treat," he told her.

She opened her mouth to speak, but he silenced her with a nod and quickly strode toward the counter.

In a place where you could get twenty-seven flavors of coffee from all regions of the globe (not including daily specials), she chose *a small decaf.* He'd just have to take it upon himself to expand her horizons. It'd be a dark day in Chi-Town before he stooped to order a simple House Blend.

"This is small and it's a decaf," he announced when he returned to their table, handing her the coffee with care and plunking down a bag of chocolate-chip-hazelnut cookies between them. "But it's also Kenyan, and it's noted for its distinctive berry-like undertones. Most people find it tangy. Hope you like it."

She smiled at him, and he almost burned his tongue on his tall Stockholm Roast. Yeah, he was in the mood for dark, smooth and full-bodied today. He inhaled deeply, wishing he could breathe in the scent of this woman along with his brew. She was simply lovely. He watched her take a cautious sip before pronouncing the Kenyan "quite good." Excellent. This lady was chock full of potential.

"So, you're finishing up your child psych program this spring?" he asked.

"Y-yes."

"Got a position already lined up after you graduate, or are you planning to begin a masters degree right away?"

She paused, a moment's confusion evident on her face as if she had to think hard to produce an answer. Maybe it was a distressing subject, but he couldn't figure out why.

"I'm still waiting to see what'll turn up over the summer before I make a final decision," she said finally.

He nodded. "Probably a good plan. Which age range do you eventually hope to work with? Young kids? Adolescents?" *C'mon, Charlotte. Go for the little ones.*

"I enjoy early childhood. I have the most experience with the preschool and kindergarten years, up to age six."

YES! Ten points to the woman with the chocolaty eyes. He grinned. "Terrific. Where did you get your experience?"

A shadow darkened her features and she looked almost upset. Oops. He didn't mean to insult her by probing into her academic training. He thought she'd be pleased by his curiosity.

Charlotte took her time composing a response. "I've had the opportunity to…interact with children at different ages and in a variety of settings. Schools, doctors' offices, parks, libraries, even private homes. I—I may appear young and inexperienced, but I always study my subjects carefully."

Well, shoot, now she was getting defensive. "Oh, I wasn't criticizing, Charlotte. I'm just interested in finding out more about you. You know, your background, your work style. I mean, are you Jungian or Freudian in orientation? Do you subscribe to Bruner's philosophy of child cognitive development? Piaget's? Or lean more toward Titchener and the structuralists?"

She looked at him like he was as nutty as one of the cookies. "I, um, tend to take a more eclectic approach."

"Yeah. A lot of people are doing that now."

"And what about you, Will? You said you were an attending physician at Regents. Do you have a medical specialty or do you plan to focus your training on a particular area later?"

He'd been waiting for this lead in. Hoping for it. "Well, yes, in a way. These days I spend most of my time at the hospital, in the ER, but that'll change soon."

"You're planning to relocate? Go into private practice?"

"Actually, I'm in the midst of getting a project approved that I've wanted to establish for several years now. A city health center. A clinic, basically, for low-income mothers and their children."

Her eyes widened. "And you're building this center?"

"No, the building's already there. We just need private investors and additional funding to pay for the running and staffing of the clinic."

A bewildered expression crossed her face before she managed to conceal it with a look of polite interest. Not quick enough for him to miss it, though. "You said you'd wanted to do this for years. What inspired you? Why *this* project above all others?"

Ah, she was a sharp one, but maybe too young and free-spirited to comprehend the challenges of single parenthood. It was too soon to tell her the story of his upbringing. She'd feel sorry for him or think he was— well, who knew what she'd think?

He took a deep breath. "It's an underserved population, Charlotte. So many of the mothers I see in the emergency room are alone, the child's father nowhere in sight. They're making a living the best they can, but there's not much opportunity or money to go around. They avoid routine healthcare if they don't have the insurance to cover it and, eventually, not just the child but the whole community suffers. It's a desperately needed service."

She looked down at her coffee, closed her eyes for a few heartbeats before looking back up at him. "I'm really impressed. What you're doing is so admirable. And, as you said, necessary."

"Thank you, but I'm not doing it alone. We're going to need a lot of good people to pull this off. People who care about other people. People with specialties in areas like…well, like yours."

He watched her head shoot up again, the startled glance she tried to camouflage with a rapid head nod. "Certainly you mean people more experienced than *me*. A project like that requires—"

"No, I mean people *exactly* like you. And, as you said, you study your subjects carefully. We'll need observant, hardworking doctors, nurses, nutritionists and child psychologists, among others, to be able to offer the kind of holistic, quality care we'd like to provide. I'm already beginning to review applications and, if you're interested, I'd love to take a look at your résumé sometime, too."

He knew by the caged-rabbit look on her face that he was moving too fast. He forced himself to sit back, sip his coffee, change the subject. "Anyway, just an idea to consider. And, though the clinic is something I'm passionate about, these cookies are a close second." He opened the paper bag and held it out to her.

She took one and bit into it. "Mmm," she said. "Wonderful."

A few crumbs clung to the corners of her lips, and he was surprised by his temptation to reach over and brush them away. But his own good sense and a warning look in her expression held him back. A whole lot was at stake here. He needed to tread more carefully than he'd been.

He watched her chew her cookie. She nibbled slowly, the corners of her mouth rising ever so slightly by the third bite. Something elusive lurked behind her eyes as well, a twinkling look that surprised him when her gaze met his.

"So, Will," she said between bites four and five, "what led you to Lady Catherine's Love Match Website? You're clearly an intelligent, attractive man with noble career plans and great taste in cookies." She grinned more broadly at him now. "You'd need little else to recommend you. Why go to all the trouble of joining an Internet matchmaking service? Why not just hang around bakeries or coffee shops like this one and look for love?"

He figured answering, *Because I made a bet I had to win*, wouldn't impress her the way he needed to. "Uh, because I spend a lot of time working," he said, which wasn't a total lie. "Meeting people takes time and energy. Plus it's hard to know if someone you meet in passing has a similar relationship objective or if that person's just playing games."

He almost bit his tongue at his own hypocrisy on that line, but he studied her reaction. She was scrutinizing his every move.

***

Beth observed the Good Doctor from dark head to pricey-leather toe. His pose so casual, his face so open. Here was a guy who had nothing to hide. And why should he?

He was thirty-two and drop-dead gorgeous.

He spoke in the rich tones of a man accustomed to privilege, and he had expensive tastes to match.

He was a full-time physician with a great career already going, plus plans to move ahead with an altruistic project that she knew firsthand was badly needed.

He made her reasons for being here seem as petty and self-serving as they were. She was guilty as accused: a game-player. If he knew the truth about her, he wouldn't want to spend another two minutes in her company, let alone want her to join his clinic's team.

She tried to remember the categories from her "stereotypes" list:

Ambitious? Yes.

Physically stronger? Oh, yes.

Assertive, critical, competitive? Certainly assertive, yes. More information needed on critical and competitive.

Values the rational over the emotional? This one should be clear-cut, and yet…a clinic for low-income mothers and their children? He didn't come across as coldly logical or cutthroat enough to score high there, but she'd have to dig deeper to know for sure.

"What about you?" he asked. "With all those

university guys out there, why search for your Perfect Match off campus?" The corners of his lips twitched and the dimple in his right cheek became more pronounced.

"I—I, um—" she stammered. "I guess I couldn't find the kind of person I was looking for there."

"Someone who could match your softball skills?"

"What?" Her softball skills were atrocious.

"You said in your first email how much you enjoyed playing softball. Couldn't find anyone on campus to play with?"

Oh, boy, he remembered everything. Beth had no honest answer readily available, so she just laughed.

"Hey, with the weather warming up, maybe we could catch a Cubs game at Wrigley Field some—" His smart phone dinged. "Damn. It's probably…" He read the number. "Yeah, sorry. I'm being paged and have to get back." He gave her an apologetic glance and rose from his seat. "That's the disadvantage of being on call."

He said more things about the hospital, but she let her mind wander. Whew. End of date. She'd lived through it, thankfully. Only she didn't get as much information as she needed. Maybe if she got him to write down his thoughts. She could send him a really long email this weekend and—

"…so, what do you say, Charlotte?"

Huh? "I—um, pardon? What was that?"

"I said, how about dinner on Friday night? Luigi's?" He sent her a smile that made her stomach melt to her toenails.

"*This* Friday?" Only *three days* from now. Her mind flew to the commitments she had lined up for the week. Other than needing someone to watch Charlie, she could probably swing it, but it still wouldn't be easy with work and school obligations. "Well, I think I could do that," she said slowly. What was she saying? What was she doing? And, oh, brother, what was she possibly going to wear?

"Great. How's six? I could pick you up at your pl—"

"*No!* I mean, thanks, but I'll probably need to run some errands first, so why don't I just meet you there."

He reached down and softly touched her shoulder. "It's a date."

***

Will sped to the hospital, glad no cops were running radar in the vicinity. He marveled over Charlotte Lucas. Amazing woman. Truly. She'd made him wish he didn't have a job to do. Wish he could've been completely candid. A pang of well-deserved guilt socked him in the gut.

Aw, man. He *liked* her.

Well, that could only spell disaster. If she knew what his motives had been, she might very well despise him.

After shoving his hard-earned, steel-blue Ferrari into park, he burst into the ER and called out to the head nurse. "Who came in?"

The white-haired lady tossed him a clipboard and pointed toward Exam Room 1. "Lydia Jenkins and her eight-month-old. High fever. Abdominal pain. Raspy cough. May be pneumonia."

Worry gripped his heart and squeezed. "The mom or the baby?"

"Both," she said.

He rushed in the room, taking in the disheveled appearance of the nineteen-year-old mother and her squalling infant. "Hey, darling," he said to Lydia, placing his fingers on the pulse points of her wrist. "When did all this start?"

"Maybe 'bout two weeks ago," she whispered,

clearing her throat as a cover, it seemed, for her coughing. "Thought it was just a bad cold. Wouldn't go away. Then Brittany got it."

He brushed some dark blond hair off her forehead and patted her shoulder before sliding over to examine the baby girl. No question about it, this child knew something bad was going down. Sobs wracked her small, pale body, and he could tell every breath was a labored wheeze.

"She gonna be okay, Dr. Darcy?" Lydia asked. "She just needs some medicine, right?"

Will listened to the baby's chest through his stethoscope. Born three weeks premature and having a low birth weight kept Brittany in the high-risk category for complications such as these.

"Antibiotics should help," he reassured her, but he'd known Lydia since her third trimester. Injections and a few pills wouldn't solve a thing long term.

He didn't need to overanalyze the chart. She'd barely received any prenatal checkups because she didn't have a job, couldn't afford the insurance premiums and hadn't been aware then of the free services available to her. No father around, of course. Parents too far out of the picture to assist. The baby needed better care than what Lydia could provide in order to grow into a healthy adult. The poverty cycle set them up and perpetuated the problem time and again.

He scribbled out a couple prescriptions, giving Lydia samples of each medication from the hospital stash so she'd have fewer to buy. He then administered the first liquid dose to the infant.

"Rest up, darling," he told Lydia. "I'm not discharging you two until after dinner, so use the next few hours to catch a nap and eat a something healthy. You might be in for a long night once you leave. I'll send a nurse down in a bit with some formula for Brittany, too."

Gratitude filled the girl's eyes. "Thanks, Doc."

Will scrambled through his next set of patients still thinking about Lydia and her daughter. It led him to other thoughts. On his first break, he reached for the phone and punched in a familiar number.

"Hey, there, Mom. How are you?"

"In a flutter! Did you see *Oprah* this morning?" She paused unnecessarily. He knew she knew the answer. "Well, anyway, there was this whole segment on radical home transformations. 'Backyard makeovers,' she called it. These experts came into some old couple's house and just turned their crummy lawn into a Japanese garden. Incredible. And now I've got so many ideas."

"Wow. That's great news." He thought of his mother's distinguished Cape Cod in the upscale Pemberley Park neighborhood that he'd helped her select and pay for. Lawns around there were manicured as diligently as a Hollywood starlet's fingernails.

"Well, yes. I called Home Depot and that nice college boy down the street—you know, the paralegal's son? He's there picking up some things for me right now. He's going to help me lay down the stone footsteps this afternoon."

"Stone footsteps?"

"I'm going for the 'English' look," she said, as if that explained everything. To him it sounded like the 'graveyard' look.

"Wow," he said again.

"Once I have it all done, you'll have to come over for tea and crumpets. Or maybe raspberry scones would be better. You could bring a girlfriend?" Will didn't miss the hopeful note in his mother's voice, nor could he overlook her desire to recreate a page from her favorite childhood book, *The Secret Garden*.

His thoughts strayed to Charlotte Lucas again, this time imagining her meeting his mom. It was always his biggest test for any woman he'd dated, not that many girlfriends had gotten that far. But Charlotte had real promise. He hoped she might see behind the middle-aged-lady façade and view the wonderful woman his mother was inside.

Few twentysomethings he'd encountered were genuinely good with the older generation, but anyone involved in his life would have to treat his mom well. In his book, she was on par with Wonder Woman.

"Tea sometime sounds like a great plan, Mom."

"Good. Oh, gotta go, honey. I hear the neighbor boy in the drive."

He hung up. Only three days until Friday. Bet aside, he couldn't wait. If he'd known a lady like Charlotte was out there, Bingley might not have had to bribe him into trying this Love Match thing.

Will envisioned himself and Charlotte together.

Him: Working at the clinic, helping patients, giving medical treatments, being able to share his knowledge with mothers in a way that made a difference.

Her: Working nearby, offering encouragement and insight, then providing ideas to emotionally support the children of these mothers.

What a team they'd make.

With no dependents, no major outside commitments, nothing to distract them, they could really do some work that mattered. And maybe, just maybe, she'd be glad he hadn't chosen her for the typical male reasons. Glad he wanted more than a woman with merely natural charm and good looks—though she had those, too—but also someone whose lifestyle would mesh perfectly with his because their specific interests and living circumstances lined up. As a couple, they'd be on the same page. Share the same worldview.

Yeah.

She'd definitely appreciate his foresight.

CHAPTER THREE

"Jane just called for you," Beth's coworker Abby announced on a fast pass through the office, long blond hair flying like a cape behind her. "Said she needed to talk with you before you took another breath."

Abby, having been at the social work agency for over a decade, knew everything and everyone tangentially associated with the place. Beth's friendship with Jane was reason enough for Abby to take an interest in the phone call and in the person who made it.

"Impatient one, that Jane," Robby, her Jamaican-American colleague, said with a shake of his dreadlocks.

Beth had just returned from a visit to Anna Marie Dermott's apartment and felt she could live without more verbal ping-pong this afternoon. Her social-work predecessor had rightly described the woman as "cantankerous." Beth preferred serving the elderly to any other population, but this lady made more demands than a toddler at Toys 'R' Us.

Still, Beth knew her best friend didn't take well to being ignored. She picked up the phone, knowing a lecture was coming, and dialed Jane's cell.

"What do you think you're doing?" Jane exploded, living up to her redheaded temperament. "Leaving me an email like that—*after the fact!* No advanced warning. No plans to fill me in on what happened with Number 49. You call this behavior *friendship?*"

Beth squeezed her eyes shut and grimaced. She'd thought of little else but Dr. William Darcy for twenty-four straight hours, but admitting this to Jane would be dangerous. Jane would see nothing wrong with finding him cute, would even encourage a get-together or two for research—alias firmly in place, of course. But to really fall for the guy? Jane would have her neck.

"It all just came about really fast," she said, remembering Will's dazzling smile, generous spirit and sharp mind. "I'd planned to call you right away, but Charlie had a project for school that we needed to work on Monday night, and I can never talk when he's there. And last night, by the time I finished the extra reports for work, it got too late and so…anyway, that's why I emailed. I'm sorry I didn't tell you about meeting Will yesterday."

"You *should* be sorry," Jane said. Beth knew she was trying her best to sound severe, although her friend's half giggle on the line spoiled the effect. "I was deprived of all the pre-date anticipation and study-related speculation."

"Who's Will?" Abby asked, eavesdropping without apology, eyebrows raised.

Beth glanced at her and shrugged. "Just a guy."

On the phone Jane all but squealed with sarcasm. "Now he's just a *guy*. Heck, no. Better tell her he's *Your Destiny*. Tell her you've found your *Perfect Love Match*."

"I'm not telling her that."

"What aren't you telling me?" Abby put her hands on

her hips in a maternal pose and looked irritated.

"You got yourself in big trouble, lady," Robby said.

"We'll talk about this later, Jane. I've got to go. Now."

"I'm bringing dinner," she said, giving a last, indignant huff. "Plan to divulge every analytic detail."

***

Charlie must have been waiting behind Mrs. Moratti's door. When Beth knocked, he jumped out at her.

"Mommmmmeeee!" The three-foot-seven body flung itself full force, squeezing her middle tight with wiry, six-year-old arms. She buried her face in his hair and inhaled. He smelled distinctively of *boy*: No-Tears shampoo plus fruit snacks plus grass and mud. Her Charlie.

"How did school go this morning, baby?"

"Good. We made caterpillars today." He grinned and pulled a multicolored, construction paper figure out of his Spiderman backpack. It vaguely resembled a leggy insect. "And we watched some cocoons in our tank and drew pictures of 'em, but not even one hatched into a butterfly yet. It was Mikey Rodrigo's birthday, so we also got cupcakes with sprinkles and jellybeans on top. But I took off my jellybeans 'cuz they were green and that color's icky."

Beth exchanged an amused glance with Mrs. Moratti, the kind woman who collected Charlie from the bus stop each day at noon and acted as his stand-in grandmother with ample hugs and cookies. "How about here? Everything go well?"

The older lady nodded. "Buona," she said with her heavy Italian accent. "S'alright today. No problemo. Snack already, at two. One video, then some PBS." She smiled, her eyes so warm and compassionate. Her adult sons lived far away now, but they always came back to

32

visit. Mrs. Moratti was a love magnet.

The gray-haired woman patted the top of Charlie's head in a gentle, almost reverent manner. "Just-a one accident this afternoon. Under the table and then—*bump.*"

Beth looked Charlie over. He seemed unfazed. If she'd known a kindergartener could be so uncoordinated, she'd have given him Klutzy as a middle name instead of Samuel, after her nimble grandfather. Then again, considering her own graceless moves at the Koffee Haus yesterday, the kid came by the trait honestly.

She thanked Mrs. Moratti with a quick embrace before leading Charlie to their apartment.

It didn't take long. Four doors down the hall, on the right-hand side, the name Bennet was painted on a little blue plaque. Home sweet home.

"What's for dinner, Mommy?" Dark eyes looked up at her with their undaunted optimism and trust in her ability to provide. She glanced apprehensively at the cupboards, knowing they were down to their last few boxes of noodles. Then she remembered.

"Oh, I don't know, actually. Auntie Jane is coming over." She snuck a peek at her watch. "Probably in about a half hour or so. She's surprising us with dinner."

"Goody! I love her ideas. Think she'll bring us McDonald's again? Or maybe meatballs from her freezer?"

"It's always a mystery with Auntie Jane."

Charlie sniffed the air in anticipation. "I know she's not my real Auntie, but she's so awesome."

And more than a little crazy. Beth smiled. "She sure is," she agreed, meaning it. "Now, go play until she gets here."

Twenty-five minutes later, Jane marched in without

preamble and plopped a large, veggie-loaded pizza on the chipped Formica table. The heavenly scent wafted up and made Beth's eyes water.

Jane seemed unaffected by the aroma. A burning sense of focus hovered above her like a spotlight, though. The intensity powerful, the curiosity unconcealed in her expression. She eyed Beth with arched brows throughout dinner, but showed considerable restraint until later, when Charlie was safely engrossed with his miniature cars two rooms away.

"Well?"

"Well, what?" Beth said, stalling.

Jane sighed and held up a finger for each of five questions. "Is he a dimwit? Was he as attractive in person as he seemed online? Did he make you laugh? Make you glad you only have to put up with him until you finish your project? Ask you out again?"

Beth considered the questions. "No. Yes. Yes. No. Yes."

Her friend squinted then focused on the one Beth wished she could've sidestepped. "*When* are you going out again?"

"Friday. Luigi's."

"*This* Friday?"

"That's what I said when he asked. But I'm thinking maybe I should cancel. Except I still have a few questions about him. Some things I need to straighten out."

Jane shot her a direct look. "Questions about your *project*, right? Not about the man himself?"

"Right. The project."

Leaning forward across the white tabletop, Jane gave her a long, assessing stare. She crossed her arms. "Shoot, Beth. I can't believe it. You like him, don't you?"

It was no use hiding things from Jane. She was too

perceptive, and she knew her too well. Beth sighed and nodded.

"That's bad."

"I know." Beth shifted in her seat, the edge of the old wood chair biting into her thigh. She needed new furniture. She needed new everything.

"So, what then? Are you going to tell him who you really are?"

"I don't know yet. I'm hoping, once we get to talk more in person, one of two things will happen. Either he'll reveal himself to be an insincere, unpleasant man, despite my positive first impression, and I'll no longer be intrigued, or he'll be as interested in my real occupation and my real life as he is in my made-up one."

"He asked you questions about child psych?"

"Oh, yeah. He seemed delighted by 'my' major. Fascinated, even. Asked me about Piaget. It was weird. I'm always impressed by your field and everything, but you know I'd rather work with older people any day."

"*That's* what's weird." Jane shook her head. "You and all your geriatric pals. You've got an old soul, Beth Ann."

"Don't start on me. And then there's his whole clinic thing, like I told you in the email." Beth got up and tossed out the sauce-stained napkins then put away the leftover pizza. "He's so…principled. How can I face a guy who thinks I could be a partner in his project when, in reality, I'm the kind of person he's trying to help?"

"Maybe he'll be impressed by your hard work and dedication to Charlie. People's views are changeable, you know, and we all have a shot at learning and growing. Maybe he'll see how much you've had to overcome and will admire you for it."

"So, you think if I told him the truth now and explained my reasons, maybe he'd forgive me for having lied to him?"

"Maybe. Maybe not. But how long can you live with the alternative?"

Beth grimaced.

Jane's lips twisted into one of her trademark smirks. "You never listen, do you? I told you, get the information and get out. That's what *I* did with my project. But what do you do? Secretly meet with the guy. Find him so very likable and intelligent. Start seeing potential in him. Actually *believe* Lady Catherine, for goodness sake!" She buried her freckle-dusted face in her palms. "Truly, you are not cut out for deception."

"You forgot to say that he's humorous, handsome and honorable."

"You neglected to mention those traits in your email," Jane said, giving a resigned sigh. "Well, I guess I know what I'm doing Friday night."

Panic caught in Beth's throat. "You're not planning on—"

"Oh, you bet I'm planning on it." Jane leveled a mock-supercilious gaze at her. "Someone's got to help you get out of the messes you get into."

The thought of Jane invading Luigi's and confronting Will there or anywhere made goose bumps jig up and down on her skin. "Please tell me you're not going to—"

"Help you find a dress?" Jane supplied, eyeing Beth's off-the-rack, discount-store outfit. "Absolutely. Watch Charlie so you can straighten things out with your 'Perfect Match'? Can't think of anything I'd rather do." She glanced toward the cupboard. "Now, have you got any dessert on hand, or do I need to take care of everything?"

***

"So, what made you choose medicine as your

profession?" Beth asked Will as they talked over dinner on Friday. "There are so many 'helping' occupations, why that one specifically?"

She crinkled the linen napkin on her lap, out of Will's view, and tried to concentrate on her stuffed manicotti oozing with delicious ricotta and mozzarella. The pungent smell of oregano threatened to overpower her, but she smiled at him and hoped she looked calm and in control.

"It's very immediate. Very direct," he said. "I guess you could say I've never been satisfied to help only behind the scenes."

"You wanted to be where the action was?"

"Yeah. But you must be that way, too. Using your knowledge to treat your young patients' minds. Having a profound impact on the quality of their lives. Being *right there* to assess and assist."

"But teachers do that also," she said then, almost holding her breath, added, "and so do social workers."

He frowned. "That's not the same thing at all." He chewed a heaping forkful of vegetable lasagna and swallowed it down with a gulp of sparkling apple cider. "Teachers are on a similar track, perhaps, in that what they do is direct. The good ones are disseminators of information and aid, when they can be. But they're like ER docs all the time, basically working triage in overcrowded classrooms. Social workers—" he grimaced. "They're a different story altogether."

Her heart pounded in time to the piped-in restaurant music, lyric-less but with an unrelenting beat. "How so?"

"They're coordinators. Cruise directors. They assign people to other people." He appeared annoyed or, worse, disgusted. "Sure their skills might benefit a select few. Sometimes. But it's in an indirect manner. A lot of them cause more trouble than they solve."

She lost her ability to speak for several seconds, watching as inexplicable anger streaked like a lightning flash across his face. He downed the rest of his cider and shook his head. "Bad experiences, I guess," he said.

Her fingertips tingled. Apprehension could reach the extremities with remarkable speed. "What about for low-income mothers? The women at your future clinic? You don't think a social worker could help them in any way?" She squeezed the napkin again. She and Charlie owed so much to the kindness of social workers.

He laughed without humor. "Hell, no. You're so entrenched in the ethics of your own field, you don't even realize how pitiful most of those people are." He took his final bite of lasagna, swiped at his mouth with his napkin and tossed it on the table next to his plate with a dramatic flick of his wrist.

"I'm telling you, most social workers are a detriment to mothers going through a rough time. They offer a few handouts in one breath and, in the next, threaten to take their children away. In abuse or addiction cases, a social service agency has no choice but to step in, but in so many instances the mother's only crime is poverty. To add heartbreaking fear to her concerns is immoral. And don't even get me started on the treatment of the elderly. That's downright criminal."

Criminal? She thought of the hours she'd spent working late, compiling services just to assist Anna Marie Dermott, despite the woman's crotchety attitude. Beth knew the lady had starved for years—not for food but for companionship and caring. In the two hours Beth spent with her this week, she'd managed to get the older woman to talk long and deep enough so she could find out what was really troubling her. She'd dug beneath the lady's belligerent veneer to unearth the true pain and need.

Beth had a hard time masking the growing dislike she felt for Will Darcy at that moment. Not even attempting to finish her manicotti, she shot him a tight smile. "Excuse me. I need to use the ladies' room."

"Would you like some coffee, Charlotte?"

Charlotte. Hearing the name jarred her yet again. But this was her own darned fault. What was she thinking getting involved with this guy at all? "No, thanks. No coffee for me." She escaped to the restrooms.

With her back pressed against the locked stall door, she dashed away tears of anger with her sleeve. Well, with Jane's sleeve.

All the trouble she'd gone to for this evening! Borrowing Jane's best black dress. Scrimping on daily expenses and skipping lunch for three days to have enough money on hand to cover her portion of the dinner bill. Sacrificing a cozy Friday night with Charlie...and for what? To spend it getting insulted?

The worst of it was that a hope she'd been afraid to name had been shattered. Despite all logic to the contrary, she'd wanted, almost expected, the fairy tale. To find her Perfect Match regardless of the odds against it. What woman didn't? But this situation was futile. Nothing could redeem the relationship now, even if she confessed who she truly was.

Well, let's face it, especially then.

She sniffed and pulled out her nearly forgotten stereotypes list from her purse. He'd sidetracked her again, this time by his opinions and insinuations about her real profession. Now she'd have to try to ignore her instinct to run home and, instead, direct her full attention to gaining the last of the information for her project.

Five minutes later, dry-eyed, she returned to the table.

"I've taken care of the bill," Will said. "Sorry if I got on my soapbox before. Your questions just touched an old nerve, but I didn't mean to take my frustrations out on you." He smiled at her pleasantly, as if he hadn't just annihilated the secret romantic fantasy of her heart. A dream even *she* knew was too dumb to admit aloud.

"I—um, it's all right. Thank you for dinner, but you should have let me contribute. May I at least leave the tip?"

"Absolutely not. But I'll let you buy me a cookie." He grinned again, broader this time so his dimple showed, and he held out his hand to her. "What do you say we walk? I know a good place a few blocks from here."

She reluctantly put her palm in his, surprised by the warmth of his fingers. He squeezed her hand in a gentle, compassionate way she didn't want to appreciate. It comforted her nevertheless.

When they were out on the sidewalk, the sun's last light casting an orange glow on everything, she inhaled the sweet spring air and took in the sight of his dark hair tinged with reflected gold highlights. She sighed.

Okay, enough procrastinating.

She had to address some of the tougher issues brought to light by past gender-research studies. She just wished her leading query didn't have to be one with so much personal meaning for her.

"So, I know you feel passionately about helping single mothers and their children," she said. "Did you ever find yourself involved in a relationship with a single mom? A good friendship or a romance? Or is your understanding of the situation primarily based on professional experiences?"

She waited for his response, trying to read the cryptic expression on his face without success. This was a crucial gender-role question. Research indicated that for reasons predominantly biological as well as social, men had a tendency to avoid relationships where they had to raise another man's offspring. Will Darcy's Love Match profile had said "No Dependents," so she figured he'd shied away from women with children in the past.

"I have a great deal of personal as well as professional experience, Charlotte."

Beth felt her jaw drop, and she had to consciously instruct it to close. So, he'd tried dating single mothers before, had he? Tried and, evidently, failed.

"I very much want to help mothers and children in need, especially low-income, single moms," he said. "But that's not a romantic circumstance I want to be involved in myself."

"Because of the mothers or because of the children?"

"Both."

"W-why? Do you consider it a moral issue? Women shouldn't get divorced or have children out of wedlock? Or is it because of more practical concerns—like raising another man's child?"

His grip on her hand tightened as he swiveled her around to face him. A momentary panic shimmied down her spine and settled in the arches of her feet. She'd be ready to spring away in an instant if she needed to.

Only, she knew she wasn't afraid of him but, rather, of her unexpected, unwanted attraction to him.

She caught his expression, noticing the upward curve of his lips, the tilt of his brows, the amused glint in his eyes. Will was laughing at her. Silently maybe, but *still*. How dare he—

"Did anyone ever tell you that you ask a lot of questions?" He tenderly pulled her to him, the front of her borrowed dress grazing against his navy sport coat.

His cologne tickled her nostrils. He smelled as she'd always imagined a Caribbean evening might. A wonderful, spicy scent.

He bent his head toward her, his lips hovering mere inches from her nose. She could see the bristly shadow on his chin and a hairline scar above his left temple. She reached out to trace it. Those clear blue eyes pierced her with calm reassurance.

"I've wanted to kiss you since Tuesday," he murmured, his breath a whisper against her skin.

She leaned in even closer.

"It may be customary to wait until the end of the date but, as you know, I'm an impatient man who likes be where the action is." He unfurled a cautious smile. "Do you have any objection to my moving up the timetable a bit?"

With him so near, smiling at her with an uncommon, respectful restraint, Beth didn't object to anything at all. The moment she shook her head, Will's lips came down to meet hers.

CHAPTER FOUR

Will forced himself to hold back, even as he kissed her. He didn't want to scare her off, not this soon, not now when he found himself liking her so much. But he couldn't help but admire her laugh, her smile, her beautifully plump lips. Natural, no Botox injections, he was sure of it.

This Charlotte Lucas was pure woman.

The kind of woman who brought out the protective male instinct in him.

She sighed, a breathy exhale coming from somewhere deep within her. He pulled her even closer, held her even tighter.

For a moment she squeezed him tight, too, but then, abruptly, she pushed away.

"What's wrong?" he asked.

"Nothing."

"What do you mean nothing? You jumped away from me like I had the West Nile Virus. Did I hurt you? Accidentally cut off your circulation?"

"No."

He felt a sharp pang of worry. Perhaps he'd misread her reaction to him. He was usually good at gauging a woman's interest, but maybe he'd been wrong this time. "Then was it something I said?"

"No, Will. But I—" Her lovely lips quivered with nervousness. "I need to take everything very slowly."

He blew out half a lungful of air. Dang. Despite his determination not to, he'd pushed her too far, too fast anyway.

"Of course we can take things slow." He reached for her arm again to continue their walk to the bakery, but she flinched as if his touch had scalded her.

Two steps forward, one step back. What an idiot he was. When would he learn to keep his enthusiasm in check?

"Listen, Charlotte—" She shot him another worried look. What? Now he couldn't even say her name? "If you want to skip the cookies, we don't have to go on. To be honest, it was just an excuse to spend a little more time with you."

She glanced down and away from him then shook her head as if in answer to some private question.

"I'd like to get you a cookie," she said. "I suppose I owe you at least that much." When she faced him again, he noticed a telltale glittering in her cocoa-colored eyes. Tears not fully formed, maybe, but still it was evidence of some real hurt. He hoped he hadn't been the cause of her pain.

He halted. He had to. "You don't owe me a thing, do you hear? Nothing. Being with you tonight has been a pleasure—all mine. You don't have to pay me back for dinner in cookies, kisses or anything else." He watched her take this in, but she remained silent, impassive.

The sun had finally dipped below the horizon, leaving

only a few lonely streaks of pink before the gray took over. He couldn't believe he was getting involved like this. Cripes, he hardly knew the lady and already his emotions hung on whatever her next words would be. He waited for them to come, cursing the shadows that kept him from reading her expression more accurately.

"Thanks for saying that," she whispered finally. "But I'd still like to get those cookies if…if you want."

Relief flooded through him like a whitewater rapid. "I want."

"And Will? You should know—" She took a breath so long and excruciating that it practically stopped his pulse. "It was a wonderful kiss. Really."

He offered his hand to her in response, not having the first clue if she'd actually take it now. When she slipped her fingers next to his, entwining them, he released a breath he hadn't realized he was holding. His heart soared at the feel of those brave little fingers, and he squeezed them gently to thank her for trusting in him again. But, man, this was crazy. Who the hell felt this way about a woman this soon?

All he knew for sure was this: In the space of a few minutes, he'd passed some test of fire with her, moved to a new level and wormed his way nearer to her trust. He wasn't sure where they were now or why she'd been so skittish but, regardless, they were closer than when they'd started the night. And for him, that knowledge changed everything.

After a few moments of companionable silence, he heard her inhale next to him. It was the kind of breath that meant a big question was coming.

"What?" he said.

She squinted at him, wearing an expression that no man, no matter how well educated, could read. "You still haven't answered the question I asked you before. The one about why you wouldn't get involved with a single mother."

She took an inordinate amount of interest in this subject. Had she guessed his background somehow? He listened to the clicking of her black heels as she walked, admiring the rhythm, before he replied. "You mean, if I hesitated to get involved because I think it's a moral issue or because it's a problematic childrearing one?"

"Right."

"Yes and no to both." About this, at least, he'd have to come clean with her. "No matter what anyone says, or how society's changed in recent decades, there's still a moral element to it. Children without fathers present still have a stigma stamped on them. One that's hard to live down. They know something's missing and, let's face it, it is."

"But the woman isn't entirely to blame there."

"No, of course not, but when she seeks a relationship with another man, the new guy always has to wonder if she's looking for a soul mate for herself or a father for her kid. No one—male or female—wants to be the second string. The B team."

He saw her consider this and nod. "I see. So this has to do with male pride. Needing to be the first, the only, the best. The leader of the pack when it comes to *your* woman." He detected more than a smidgen of bitterness in her voice. "And, thus, even an abandoned woman and her offspring are considered possessions of the original man. Leftovers, basically, from the vantage point of any other man who might come along later."

"I'm not saying it's a nice way of looking at it, but your inference isn't entirely untrue."

She released his hand. They'd arrived at the bakery,

but she resisted taking a step inside. For whatever reason, she was determined to bring this conversation to its inevitable conclusion. Sooner or later he'd have to help her make the final deductive leap.

"Look," he said, "children without fathers bring certain issues with them. A kind of emotional baggage you don't get when you have your own kids. They're looking for things in the new man that they dreamed about or wished for and, at the same time, they've got all these fears that they'll lose primacy in their mother's lives or that the new man will resent them for the role they used to have."

"So, the burden of being the new man is too weighty, is that it?" she said. "It's simply too much *work* to have to wade through any of these issues with the children, and the woman who was the initial attractor is probably not worth all the fuss anyway?"

In the entrance light, he could see the heightened color of her cheeks. Her eyes simmered with anger. A woman feeling solidarity toward other women, he figured.

He tilted his head to the side, taking in her slender figure and her dreadfully rigid posture. He wished she'd let him lighten things up, but the conversation wasn't heading in that direction. Not by a long shot.

"You think I'm a real jerk for being this honest, don't you?" He paused to let her digest his question. She narrowed her dark eyes at him but said nothing.

"I was called a jerk a few times when I was a kid," he continued, "but mostly I was called a bastard. And that was hard to defend against when, technically, it was the truth."

***

Beth swallowed.
Twice.

Did he really mean what she thought? "Will, are you saying your mom—"

"Yeah. Out of wedlock pregnancy. And I lived in a time and place where only a handful of kids in my whole grade school even had divorced parents. I grew up making up stories about my 'real' father, pretending he was a war hero who died when, really, my mom couldn't tell me a damn thing about him. He was just a louse who promised her the moon and stars in the backseat of his car and then didn't stick around to even find out my name a few months later."

"Did she have any support? Did her parents—your grandparents —help her out at all?"

"Oh, no. She was tossed out of the house with just a bus ticket to get her to a bigger town. They told her good luck and not to come back there without a husband."

She sank into a bench near the front door to the bakery, her anger at Will having dissipated like twilight's mist in the night air. She motioned for him to join her. He squeezed into the space to her right, and she reached over and placed her hand on his.

"I'm sorry."

He shrugged. "Not your fault, sweetheart."

"She must have done all right for herself, though. I mean, Will, look at you. You're a doctor. You've 'made it,' so to speak. Any mother would be very proud."

"She is, but she didn't have it easy." He drew in a labored breath. "She took her parents' last words to heart and found herself a couple of different husbands along the way. Not having money growing up or not feeling like I had a complete identity was one thing. Having two stepdads who hated me was another."

He balled the hand beneath hers into a fist as if preparing for a battle that had long since ended.

"Albert Darcy was the name of my mom's first husband. He legally adopted me and then ignored me for four years. Once he left for good, Mom remarried and later divorced Steve Olinger, who wouldn't play catch with me in the yard if he hadn't been bribed with a beer first." He gave her a hard, direct look. "And I know that for a fact."

She hated to think how a young boy would come to know something as awful as that. It would rip her apart to witness Charlie being treated so callously by anyone. She'd never get involved with a man who couldn't regard her son as his own. A man who wouldn't love him or who would treat him as if he were another man's "mistake."

"Will—"

"Hey, enough about all this." Though his voice fluttered with forced lightness, steel finality was the core underneath. There would be no returning to this topic tonight. And she knew it, even before the grown man—with the little boy's hurt still burning inside—jumped up and said, "I'm ready for my cookie now, and I want a big one."

***

"Did you tell him your real name?" Jane asked a few hours later when Beth stepped through the door and kicked off her high heels.

"Nope."

"Did you ask him what he thought of social workers?"

"Yep."

"And?"

"Negative reviews."

"Jeez. What about single mothers?"

Beth shook her head. "It's a definite problem."

"Well, shoot. So that probably ends it, right?" Jane gave her an expectant look.

"Probably."

The auburn brows jerked upward as though marionette strings controlled their movements. Jane's lips twisted into a grim line. "I don't like the sound of this. What's keeping you holding on to him? You can't possibly still need more information for the project, can you?"

A sigh forced its way out of her. "Well, there's never such a thing as having too much research on hand." Beth unzipped the silky dress and stepped out of it, taking great care not to crease or tear anything. She put in on a hanger and slipped into her thin cotton nightgown while Jane bided her time nearby.

"I'm waiting for the real reason, Beth."

"In a minute." She tiptoed into Charlie's room, kissed her sleeping baby on the cheek and turned to leave, when his voice called her back.

"Mommy?"

"Yes, darling?"

"Me and Auntie Jane had fun tonight, but I missed you."

"I missed you, too, sweetie."

"Can we have Worms and Rocks for lunch tomorrow?"

Charlie's name for spaghetti and meatballs. It was a certainty that they'd stretch the last of the spaghetti through the entire weekend. And she could try to scrounge up a few meatballs for him. "Sure."

"And can we play ball outside this weekend?"

"We'll see. Now go to sleep."

When Beth reemerged, Jane had her arms crossed and her forehead creased in concentration. "So?"

"So, since you're the most persistent person on the planet, Jane, it's because I've never been kissed like that. Ever."

"He kissed you?" Her blue-gray eyes widened, and her pointy little jaw dropped.

Beth made a "V" with her index and middle fingers. "Twice."

"That nice, huh?"

"It was so far beyond 'nice' I'd need a thesaurus to find a worthy adjective."

"Stupendous? Extraordinary? Astonishing? Breathtaking? Stunning? Astounding? Surprising? Remarkable?" Jane supplied with her usual, phenomenal speed.

"Now you're getting closer."

Jane squinted, her expression both serious and worried. "You'd better be careful."

Of course Beth knew she had to be careful. Charlie's father, Pete Wickham, had been the kind of kisser who made women forget their own names. But Will...he was in a class far superior to her ex-husband. If Pete was a civilian with a stun gun, Will was a Navy SEAL Special Forces commander with an M-16.

Jane left and Beth flicked off all the lights except for the one in her bedroom. Then she impulsively snatched a slim photo album off her bookshelf.

Oh, Pete. Where are you now? What are you doing? Do you ever think about us?

Opening it to the first page, she admired herself in a tea-length, cream-colored gown. Her wedding gown. Or, more accurately, her secret-elopement gown. The one she'd worn to Vegas in mid-June, eight days after her twentieth birthday, for her spontaneous, Chapel-of-Love marriage to Pete and subsequent conception of her beautiful son.

She flipped through about half of the book. She'd never looked happier. Then again, good things had a way of coming to an end, didn't they?

By the time Charlie was born the following March, Pete was thoroughly spooked by fatherhood. He was a year ahead of her in school and hung around only long enough to graduate from college that May. He contributed a couple hundred dollars to help with the hospital bill, but no follow-through on child support, no interest in bonding with his newborn son and no honoring of his wedding vows. By her twenty-first birthday, Pete was already a memory, captured only by a handful of old photographs.

Beth snapped the dusty album shut and shoved it back onto the shelf. She thought of Will. For the three-hundredth time. In less than two hours.

After he'd kissed her breathless by her car, he'd asked her out again. It was to be a midday, midweek date to an undisclosed location. A "mystery date." It was also a little tidbit of information she'd purposely neglected to tell Jane.

Why couldn't he have been more consistently stereotypical? Then she wouldn't have had to keep seeing him. She wouldn't have had to admit he had any genuine reasons for his behavior. This made her work more difficult.

She snickered. Yeah, right. The more honest question would be: Why did she ever think she could fool herself? Her final report wouldn't be academically stellar, but she knew she could muddle through it well enough now. She just enjoyed the pretense that seeing him another time was a requirement.

But it was getting ever more dangerous. Tonight,

before they parted, he'd asked for her address and phone number. "I just want to call and chat some night," he'd said, resting a casual hand on her shoulder that, nevertheless, made her pulse accelerate faster than his Ferrari.

She put him off. Told him she was rarely home, what with her many commitments and all. Said that emailing was still the quickest and easiest way to get in touch with her.

"For now, maybe," he said smoothly. "But one of these days you're going to be sitting on your sofa, sipping your orange juice and watching some boring TV show, wishing I were there to keep you company. It's a time like that when I'd call…or knock on your door and surprise you in person."

He'd be the one who'd get surprised, she thought, feeling the bleakness of their situation descend upon her. And, somehow, she doubted his reaction, once the shock wore off, would be that of overwhelming delight.

Next week, she decided. Next week she'd break things off between them.

CHAPTER FIVE

Will tapped the phone against his ear, distorting his cousin's yakking voice in the process. The grating sound was the only thing that differentiated this particular conversation from the umpteen thousand preceding it. He experimented with twisting the cord, too, but that, unfortunately, altered nothing at all.

"...and the blonde, whoa, baby! You need to meet this one. She must've been five-foot-ten at least. She models swimwear, I'm not kidding, out in New York, and her twin sister's a leading off-Broadway actress who—"

"How far off-Broadway?" Will broke in. "Like, are we talking Queens, or are we talking Quebec?"

"You're really not that funny," Bingley said, the junior-high dourness returning to his voice. "I'm only trying to help you out."

"You're not trying to help me. You're trying to amuse yourself. Anyway, I told you, I'm handling it. Look, Bingley—" He gulped some air. "I've kind of met someone." There. He'd said it. His cousin would jump all over him for details, but he had to lay down the groundwork immediately. He was cutting it close on time.

"Well, for goodness sake, Cuz, you could've told me *that* forty minutes ago."

"What? And missed the weekly recitation of the personals?"

"So, what the hell are you waiting for? What's the lucky chick like?"

Will thought of Charlotte—her warmth, her intelligence, her wise and impressive choice of profession—and smiled into the phone. "She's an angel." A lengthy silence greeted him on the line. "And, oh, she's twenty-two. Finishing up her degree in child psych. About medium height. Slim. Wavy light-brown hair. Beautiful mouth."

This stuff Bingley understood. "Well, alrighty then. Looks like you've got yourself a babe. How many dates into it are you?"

"Our third date's tomorrow. I've kept all the receipts from the first two, and I've printed out every one of her emails. I'm not ready to introduce her to you yet, but with Mother's Day weekend a month away, I figure I've got a while."

"A month's a long time, Cuz." Bingley tittered on the other end of the line. "How 'bout I up the ante a bit? Are you game?"

Apprehension shot through Will like an iodine injection. "Jeez, Bingley, don't back out on me now."

"I'm not backing out, just raising the stakes a notch. We keep the same terms as before—bring her over to my place all lovey-dovey and everything, and it better be authentic, and you get the start-up sum I promised. But with a whole month to go, I'll add this rider onto it." He chuckled. "Bring her in with an engagement ring, and I'll double the money I promised."

"An engagement ring?"

"Yeah. Yours, not some other guy's. Got it?"

"No, Bingley, I couldn't..." But even as he said it, his mind spun wildly. Double the money? That would be an enormous amount of funding. The supplies they could have on hand. The extra staff they could hire. They could install central air in the building immediately instead of waiting until next summer. It would be phenomenal. But phenomenal enough to propose marriage to a woman? Even a woman as remarkable as Charlotte Lucas? Too soon to tell.

"Think about it, Cuz," Bingley said to him in his best voice of temptation.

Will just sighed.

"Your mama would treat me like Prince Bingley himself if she knew I helped lead you to the altar."

"Crumpets may be headed your way regardless."

"What?" Bingley asked.

"Nothing."

After Will hung up on his ever-scheming, second-closest relative, he poured himself a strong cup of Vanilla Bean and settled in with the stacks of paper before him. All for the clinic. First Bingley and now the hospital board. Much as he despised social workers and the social services agencies he'd had the misfortune to deal with as a child and, later, as a doctor, he'd been given a not-so-subtle hint today that he needed to play nice with them.

Dr. Hans Emrick, sixty-one-year-old chief of staff and Swiss import, informed him that the hospital board would surely request a consulting social worker for the clinic when approval went through. *When*. That, at least, had a hopeful ring to it. Emrick gave him a number to call. Some guy Emrick said was okay. Direct line to the guy's office.

"Might as well select your own people," the older doctor told him, thrusting the slip of paper his way. "Otherwise, they'll foist someone on you, like it or not."

Will unfolded the crumpled note and glanced at the name and number. He sighed and picked up the phone.

"Chicago Social Services," the man said when he answered. "Dan Noelen speaking."

***

"I'm ninety-three if I'm a day," Lynn Hammond told Beth proudly, "but, girl, I feel like I'm only eighty."

"And you look just wonderful, too, Mrs. Hammond. How have the exercises been going?"

"Ah, the darned stroke, you know. Can't move like I done back in the '50s." She laughed, loud and hearty, then plunked her substantial body down in the wooden rocker across from where Beth sat. The older woman leaned forward, handing her a list written in large, somewhat wavering script. "There be the biggest problems I got. Don't 'spect you to solve 'em all, but some'd help a lot. Really could use them Merry Maids. Edna raved about those gals."

Beth scribbled the request down in her notebook and scanned the short list Mrs. Hammond gave her. The dear lady wasn't being demanding like Anna Marie Dermott. In fact, Lynn Hammond rarely asked for much. Just enough support to help her maintain her dignity. To allow her to feel as if she were fully capable of taking care of herself and her life.

She sipped the iced tea the woman brought in when Beth first arrived. "Yum, this is delicious."

"Well, drink up, girl. Plenty more there in the fridge for ya."

"Thank you." Beth finished making notes and returned the list to the woman. "Every request you made is reasonable and, I believe, easily achievable. I know you're up for recertification this month, so my supervisor will be contacting you soon and a full-time social worker, probably Abby, will need to oversee signing the final papers. But there shouldn't be any problem with these additions."

"Abby? That blond, nosy one, right?"

Beth laughed. "Well...um, she *is* blond."

"I thought of being blond one time." Mrs. Hammond winked and touched her tight afro curls, gray with a few hints of black. "Tried out one of them special wash-in colors. Made me look like my head was sprouting hay. 'Fraid some horse on my Uncle Manny's farm might come up to me and take a nibble." She gave a good-natured grin. "You ever try anything diff'rent, child?"

"Not with my hair," Beth admitted. *Only with my research projects.*

"Well, now, s'perimenting can be a good thing. Gerald, my first husband, he always said, "Them who don't take chances, also don't take life's best gifts. 'Course when he said it he was trying to get me to marry him." She let out a throaty laugh.

Beth joined her. "Did he manage to convince you right away?" she asked, knowing full well it was none of her business, but Mrs. Hammond didn't seem remotely hesitant to share.

"Sure did. We got hitched the next week and within a year we had our son Raymond. I be only nineteen then and not ready to be a mama, but I tell you, girl, I don't regret nothing."

Beth took a long sip of iced tea, letting the coolness of the liquid sooth a heated reaction in her brain. Her mind's question took her by surprise, and she felt it pour out of her. "But don't you sometimes wish life would've run smoother? That as much as you loved your son when he was born, being a mother would've been easier if you'd been a bit older and had experienced more of life on your own?"

Mrs. Hammond laughed. "It ain't never easy to be a mama, don't matter what age." She fiddled with a curl just above her ear and pressed her lips together. "No. Life just ain't painless. There always be some problem to face. Either bein' alone or bein' with someone. Gettin' a baby too soon. Havin' a baby who's sick or who's got problems. Havin' a baby and no good man. Makin' too many babies or not bein' able to make a baby. Always something."

Too true. Beth nodded and finished her drink. Mrs. Hammond looked heavenward and blew a kiss to the cracked ceiling.

"So, girl, you learn to deal with what gets handed down t'you. To grow up means you be honest with y'self. Face what you done, what choices you made, what you couldn't do. Be grateful for what you be given. Life don't come smooth, but you make a path, even with all them rocks in your way, that you can walk on and be proud of."

A few hours later Beth was still considering the elderly woman's words. Had she created a life for herself and Charlie that she was proud of?

She drove to the university library and parked in the lot. Not entirely was the answer to the question. Or, at least, not yet. But there was still time to change that. She had to.

She pulled a photo from her purse, a snapshot of her parents holding Charlie when he was ten months old. And she was in it also. Her younger self stood just inside the frame, a step away from the three of them, and she stared off to the side at something unknown. Had she been grateful for the blessings she'd been given?

Sometimes. Maybe not as often as she should be. Her parents, though far away geographically, were still emotionally close. She was the one who'd insisted upon independence. Love shone in their eyes at both her and at Charlie. And many people in her Chicago "family" were full of kindness and compassion. Mrs. Moratti. Jane. Dan, Abby and Robby at work.

She wondered about Will. She reached for her notes on gender-role stereotypes. Her lists. Her scribbles about the handsome doctor. In her day planner, she'd blocked out the next few hours to work on her paper, to at least get a solid head start. It needed to be written soon and turned in to Professor O'Reilly. But it was difficult to compose. The Will Darcy she'd met didn't fit neatly into a category. She was striving hard for objectivity, but he defied her expectations so far. Had she been honest with herself?

She couldn't answer this one. Didn't want to think about it. She forced herself to gather up her materials and pull the key out of the ignition, but she couldn't make herself open the car door. If she wrote this paper falsely, if she painted Will in an unfair light, that would be the absolute worst way to end this project. It would be too much—and too darned wrong—to lie not only about herself to him but also about him to others.

She stared at the library for a full minute before putting the car into gear and driving away.

***

"Charlotte Lucas, this is my mother Angela Olinger."

Beth swallowed her panic and extended her hand to Will's mom, an attractive brunette in her mid-fifties. She wore her hair in Jackie-O chic, the top of her head barely brushing against her six-foot-one son's shoulders as she reached for Beth's palm.

"It's actually Angela Kane Darcy Olinger," she said, grinning. "But please, Charlotte, call me Angie."

Beth almost winced at the "Charlotte," but tried to not let it throw her too much. After all, what was in a name? She could be open and pleasant no matter what they called her.

"It's so nice to meet you, Angie." Beth released the lady's warm fingers and looked around the cozy kitchen. This hadn't been the midweek "date" she'd expected but, then again, Will's unpredictability was, ironically, the most consistent thing about him.

Angie had the usual copper skillets, decorative sugar jars and potted ivy plants typical of an affluent household, but it was the embroidered wall hangings that drew Beth's attention. "This is beautiful," she whispered, touching one creamy fabric corner and marveling at the precise stitches that made up the design: a basket of colorful spring flowers.

Will rested his hand on her shoulder. Her pulse raced in response. "Mom made that," he said, with an affectionate glance at his mother. When he took his palm away, she felt a sudden loss.

"Well, I used to be a seamstress," Angie explained. "I just made these for fun."

"Really?" Beth said, admiring another, this one depicting a loaf of bread and some cheese on a cutting board. "They're a work of art. Every stitch is perfect."

Will laughed. "I'd never admit this at the hospital, Charlotte, but Mom can suture better than I can."

Angie shook her head and grabbed Will's chin, pulling his face down toward her. "But look at all you can do, my darling." She planted a loud kiss on his nose, and Beth felt the love flowing between them. It was the same mother-son bond she shared with Charlie.

Will gave his mom an extra squeeze then turned his blue eyes on Beth. "Mom invited us over for high tea," he said, pointing to the sliding door with a view of Angie's backyard. Woven-lace placemats and napkins decorated the circular patio table, a paisley umbrella providing shade. A sprig of baby carnations graced each setting along with fine silverware and delicate bone china with a rose pattern.

"Don't forget, there are scones, too," his mother added. "With strawberry jam and clotted cream. I hope you like English Breakfast tea, Charlotte."

Beth hadn't been served tea since she was sixteen and her own mom had taken her out for a ladies-only birthday brunch. Splurging on treats like these nowadays was out of the question. She inhaled slowly and tried to rein in a sudden sentimentality. "I'm sure I'll love it," she said, keeping her voice even. "Thank you."

"Good. Let's go outside then."

The day was sunny with a light breeze blowing off the Great Lake to their east. Beth was supposed to be in sociology class with Jane right now listening to a presentation on gender issues within foreign cultures.

Jane hadn't missed a beat when Beth called her to cancel. Beth claimed she had an appointment to go to and hoped she could get the notes later. "Sure," Jane said before hanging up. "As long as it's not a *doctor's* appointment." Beth had laughed softly but didn't answer or admit the truth. She blanched at the thought of having to fess up to her friend later.

"Is everything okay?" Will asked, pulling out one of the patio chairs for her.

"Um, yeah. Of course." She smiled at him. "Why

wouldn't it be?"

"Well, you had an odd expression—" he began.

"Will," called his mother, who'd trailed them outside with the teapot and the platter of scones. "Take this for me, would you?" She handed him the silver plate filled with lightly browned pastries. A moment later she rushed back inside to get the last few items. Fresh butter, jam, clotted cream, plus milk and sugar for the tea.

Beth hadn't eaten much for breakfast. Her stomach rumbled at the sweet aroma swirling around them. "This is lovely, Angie. Did you make the scones yourself?"

Will's mom gave a little huff before grinning at her. "Well, dear, I tried. In this month's *Woman's Day* there was a recipe for gorgeous orange-cranberry scones. Oh, you should've seen the photo. They all looked so fluffy-light in the magazine, like any minute a butterfly might spirit one away." She shook her head.

Will quirked a brow. "And yours?"

"Were like softballs. I don't know what went wrong. Three batches I tried, and not one of them was remotely flaky." She shrugged and passed Beth the platter. "These are from my favorite spot, dear, The British Bakery on Fourth and Clark. They're cinnamon-raisin."

"Well, Mom, this is pretty as a picture," Will said ever-so-sweetly as he glanced around the table. "I think *Woman's Day* should come here and photograph *you*."

His mother laughed and reached for the teapot.

"In fact," he said, jumping up, "I've got just the thing." He raced into the house.

Beth stared after him for a second before turning to his mom. "What's he going to do?"

"Oh, your guess is as good as mine." She waved Beth's question away with a flick of her wrist. "Please, let me pour you some hot tea."

Beth held her cup and saucer steady while Angie poured. She wondered if the coffee-loving doctor was trying to avoid his mother's specialty tea. "Thanks," she said just as Will returned carrying a full-sized Polaroid camera. She squinted up at him.

"It's really old and more than a little dusty," he explained. "But we still had an extra roll of film in the camera drawer, so it's loaded and ready to shoot." He tossed a triumphant grin in his mother's direction. "This is fun to use. Let's get one of you first, Mom."

Will snapped the photo and then asked Angie to take a couple of the two of them. He draped his arm over Beth's shoulders, drawing her closer to him. He smiled in his relaxed and easy way, but there was an energy in the air Beth couldn't quite identify. He watched the images develop with an intense, directed focus, as a child might.

A thought of Charlie crossed her mind. How was he doing right now? Was he feeling happy? Safe? Did he miss anything by never having had a fun Polaroid picture taken of him? She just had an ancient 35mm at home that her parents had given her as a teen. She didn't have even a cheap digital camera. Or a cell phone, so no camera app either. There were so many experiences she'd never given her little boy. Did he ever feel deprived?

Will held the pictures up for her to view more clearly. "They turned out well," he said, admiring them. "Especially considering how old this camera is. We each get to keep one." He passed the closest one over to her and stuffed his in his shirt pocket, patting it thoughtfully. "But now we'd better get to the tea or we're gonna be late."

"Of course, dear," Angie said. "What are you and Charlotte planning on doing?"

His mother glanced at them with kindly interest, but

Beth's heart was doing an aerobic dance in her chest. Yeah, what *were* they going to do?

"Well," he said, shooting Beth a sly look, "Charlotte doesn't know it yet, but I got her a surprise." He pulled two small tickets out of his wallet. "Cubs and Cardinals play at Wrigley Field in an hour and a half." He waved the tickets at her and looked pleased. His expression told her he expected nothing less from her than sheer delight.

"Wow...we're going to a baseball game?" Beth managed, trying to keep the trepidation from her voice. "That *is* a surprise."

"I knew you'd like it," Will said, nodding. "Hey, Mom, can I borrow the camera for the rest of the day? It'll be fun to snap a few more photos."

***

Will felt like Eddie Albert's character in *Roman Holiday*, secretly taking a bunch of pictures of Audrey's Hepburn's runaway princess so his newspaper buddy Gregory Peck could write that exclusive story. It was underhanded, deceitful but, in his case, absolutely necessary.

Well, there was nothing too covert about a clunky, outdated Polaroid camera, but he liked handling it better than the digital one on his smart phone. It's just that Charlotte had no idea he'd be using the photos as tangible proof to give Bingley. Anger at his cousin's game playing rose in his chest like heat off a grill. He tried to force it back down.

The only thing he'd told her about his cousin so far was that he and Bingley once fought off a jittery lizard when they were camping. Looking down at the Camera of Deception in his hands, Will figured he and the lizard should have bonded together to fight off Bingley instead.

He had already gotten a picture of Charlotte standing

by the ballpark's entrance. He bought her a "Go, Cubbies!" jersey and snapped her photo wearing that. Now it was time to capture her with some food. Most apropos would be a hotdog, but he didn't see a vendor anywhere near them.

"What's everyone doing?" she asked, glancing around Wrigley and tugging on her sleeve cuffs as if they were biting her. Spectators all around them were standing up.

"Seventh inning stretch," he said, surprised she didn't remember. He pulled her to her feet.

"Oh, that's right," she said quietly. She shot another uneasy look around the stadium.

"Don't worry. I'll bet you're a good singer."

"What?" She sounded alarmed. "We're singing?"

Just then the announcer introduced the guy who'd lead them all in "Take Me Out to the Ballgame." Will shook his head. For a ball fan, she sure didn't know much.

It confused him but, if he was honest with himself, she'd been acting more than a little strange all day. She seemed nervous when he picked her up at the Koffee Haus earlier. She wasn't too talkative at his mom's place. She fidgeted in the car ride to Wrigley. And she barely commented on any of the Cubs' plays or players. It was as if she knew something was going on behind her back. The whole ruse made him feel like a Grade-A slimeball.

Everyone started singing.

He snuck a glance at her during the "buy me some peanuts and Cracker Jacks" line. She barely mouthed the words. He felt his heart sink to his feet, and he sighed. He'd have to cheer her out of this mood, turn things around somehow. Maybe she was hungry. He reached for her hand and she jumped.

"Hey," he yelled over the loud vocals of the crowd.

"Wanna hotdog?"

She nodded but pulled her hand away. He swallowed and let her retreat from him. With the hand she'd rejected, he finally managed to flag down a vendor.

This day was turning into one long punishment. He could look at her, he could snap pictures of her, but he couldn't touch her or allow himself to get emotionally attached to her.

And, man, once she found out what he was doing with these photos, she'd probably never let him talk to her either.

***

They were back at the Koffee Haus again. Beth surveyed the parking lot and located her car. After riding around for most of the day in Will's Ferrari, her boxy eight-year-old Honda seemed uncomplicated and uninteresting.

What a day. First meeting his mom, whom she'd liked a great deal, but was he really getting this serious about her? Or was it some kind of personality test she had to pass?

And then watching three hours of baseball. Could he tell she was hopelessly lost during the game? The Cubs beat the Cardinals five to two, so the crowd went home happy. She went home with a bunch of new questions. What the heck was an RBI? Is batting "four hundred" *good*...or not? She'd never been a fan of the sport, so there was a ton she didn't know. She'd have to ask her work colleagues to explain. She knew Robby, at least, was pretty big into baseball.

Will walked her to where she'd parked. Gentlemanly of him, although it was still late afternoon and perfectly safe. She reached for the car-door handle then turned to face him, wanting him to kiss her but not wanting to appear too eager about it. He took a step forward and set his hand lightly on her left hip. Her whole side warmed to his touch.

"I'm not a stalker, you know," he said.

"What?"

"You can give me your address and phone number, Charlotte. We've known each other for long enough, don't you think? I'm not going to sneak around your place without your permission, peek into your windows or call every half hour between midnight and six to ask indecent questions."

He paused, then added with a grin, "Not that I'm not curious about you. But you have nothing to worry about. I mean, I gave you my word we'd take things slow, and I've even introduced you to my *mother*. I'm hoping you've guessed by now that I'm not a psycho, and I'm not going to do anything irresponsible."

"I—I guess I do know that," she admitted, her pulse hammering in her ears. "But the circumstances are a little complicated where I live. It really has nothing to do with you, Will. Honestly." And that was true, she realized. The problem was hers and hers alone. "I'd feel better if we kept in touch through email only for just a while longer. Please, can we do that?"

He gave her a long scrutinizing look. "Charlotte?" he said. She held her breath, afraid to move or even blink. "Please tell me the truth on this." He took a cautious step forward and leaned in.

Her heart thudded in her chest so fast she couldn't count the beats. "Of course," she whispered.

He clenched his jaw, bit his lower lip, squinted. "Are you married or engaged to someone?"

"No. No, I'm not," she answered honestly. "I'm neither married nor engaged." She almost added, *Not anymore,* but she saw the immediate effect of her words on his face. Relief rushed out of him like a wave breaking and she couldn't stand the thought of bringing back that tension.

He lifted one brow and half-grinned. "Secret boyfriend—besides me, that is?"

"No."

"Okay. In that case, I guess I'll just have to trust you until you're ready to share." He took another step forward and her racing heart stopped.

Then he kissed her softly. The kind of kiss that made her feel as though she were floating with her eyes closed, or on some chocolate high, or both. A kiss she could step into. One that embraced her as tightly as she embraced Will. She didn't want to let go.

"Up for a movie this weekend?" he said, drawing away from her only far enough to speak.

She nodded and he kissed her again. Someone in the parking lot wolf-whistled. And Beth knew Charlie and Mrs. Moratti were waiting for her return just a few miles away. And Jane would have a lecture to deliver if Beth's whereabouts were known to her. And there was still that darned paper to write and a career ladder to hop on. And she could find a thousand other reasons to follow logic and not emotion.

She ignored every one of them.

When he finally released her, Will tapped the tip of her nose with his finger. "You're a remarkable young woman, and a mysterious one. What do you have to say for yourself?"

She tried to catch her breath, but it'd run away from her somewhere between Wrigley Field and the Koffee Haus. She inhaled what air she could and said, "How about...Go, Cubbies?"

CHAPTER SIX

"What was my Daddy like?" Charlie asked again.

Beth had pretended not to hear him the first time. She'd flipped on the hot water tap in the kitchen and busied herself washing dishes. This time, with her son's head at her elbow, she couldn't ignore the question.

"Um, he was tall," Beth began, fighting a sigh. "He had blond hair, a little lighter than yours. Hazel eyes. A goofy smile. He liked sports." She paused, wondering if he'd let her stop now.

"And his name..." Charlie began.

Nope. No stopping.

"...was Pete, right?"

"Yes, sweetheart. Pete Wickham."

"But our last name is Bennet. Everyone in Mikey's family is called Rodrigo. His mom, his dad, his sister, his dog Rex—"

"Well, not every family is the same. In our case, you and I have a different last name than Pete." *Because I couldn't stand to be a Wickham anymore after he'd abandoned us.*

"Is Daddy dead?"

Beth clenched a newly rinsed dish, forcing herself to set it extra carefully in the drying rack. "No. No, he's not."

"So then why can't I see him?"

She turned off the tap and dried her hands before kneeling down in front of her little boy. "Charlie, I don't know where he is right now. I don't think he knows where we are either. And there are a lot of people in the world. Sometimes it's just too difficult to find someone again once they've moved someplace else." *Especially if a particular person doesn't look because he doesn't want the responsibility of being a father.*

"What if we moved back to where we lived when I was a baby?"

Beth thought of the cramped studio apartment near the "El" train tracks, the subsidized housing they'd lived in for two years. It made this humble apartment seem like a penthouse suite by comparison. "That place is too small for us, and Mrs. Moratti lives here. We'd really miss her if we had to move."

Her son's forehead crinkled as he considered this. "Yeah." He breathed in and out a time or two. "Maybe she could move in with us, though."

She smiled and kissed one of his creamy cheeks. "I think she likes living in her own place, but it's great having her just down the hall, isn't it?"

He nodded.

"Okay," she said. "I have a treat for you from my friend Abby at work. It's in my jacket pocket. Can you find it?"

Charlie raced out of the room and Beth closed her eyes, grateful at having changed the subject. Still, she knew she couldn't skirt the issue forever. More and more questions were coming up. More frequent and more detailed questions.

Someday she'd have to have that talk with him. The one she'd dreaded for six years already. The one that explained how she and Pete got married too young. How Pete's fears made him run away. How unlikely it would be for Charlie to ever get to know his father.

She knew Charlie would either blame her for not convincing Pete to stay or, worse, blame himself for being a major reason why Pete left.

But she wasn't going to make up stories about a dad who loved him and then died. Or a dad who went away because he needed to work to support the family and who'd someday come back. Or even a dad who'd married Charlie's mom because he'd truly loved her but left before he knew there'd be a baby. Pete hadn't truly loved her, and he knew Charlie was on the way.

About these things, Beth realized, she could never lie to her son, even if the truth really hurt. But he was still too young yet to hear the unvarnished version.

"Hey, fruit snacks." Charlie called. "Yes!"

She smiled but a droplet of bittersweet life lodged itself in her throat. Such little things still made him so happy…and that wouldn't last forever.

***

"I'd like to help you, Dr. Darcy," Will heard Dan Noelen say over the phone, "but we're very short-staffed right now. One of my most experienced social workers, Mimi Jeffries, resigned recently, and we're still trying to cover her caseload. I've got someone lined up to step into her position next month, but that young woman is still being trained, and we'll also need to hire someone new to take over the work she's been doing for us." He sighed. "As I told you the last time we spoke, it's very tight."

Will grimaced even though Noelen was only being

truthful. The guy had merely promised to check into Will's request for a consultative social worker from his department. He'd never made any promises to actually help.

"So, your saying that even by late summer, once the clinic is staffed and the supplies are in place, there's still no guarantee someone under your direction could serve as our consultant?"

There was silence on the other end of the line. Will waited, holding his breath. He knew by now that Noelen wasn't being rude, he was just thinking.

"We're at the end of April, so there's May, June, July, August," Noelen said, almost to himself. "Four months really. It's not impossible, Doc. Normally I wouldn't even consider taking on a new project at a time like this, not knowing for sure who the staff'll be come June or July. But I've got some good people in mind and, with a little luck, things'll be running smooth by the time you need us. Besides, Dr. Emrick called yesterday and put in a good word for you."

Thank heavens for Hans Emrick. Will started to feel air filling his lungs again. "Hans spoke highly of you, too, Mr. Noelen. You've worked with him before?"

"We've know each other for over a decade. He ran the ER back when my mom had her first stroke," Noelen explained. "Good guy."

Is he ever. Will agreed both silently and aloud.

"Why don't we get together in person, Doc. Bring your proposal over to the agency sometime in the next week or two. We can sit down and figure a way to work this out. We should, at the very least, be able to be a resource for you and your clinic. How's that sound?"

"Very hopeful," Will said, understanding why Emrick liked this guy and feeling less hostile toward social workers than usual. Well, this particular social worker. Nothing could change the rats he'd known in the past.

"Great," Noelen said. "Got your calendar out?"

***

Date number four, Will thought as he spotted Charlotte's serviceable but ugly green Honda in front of the Starlight Cinema. After tonight it would be four dates down and one to go with a couple weeks to spare before Mother's Day and Bingley's birthday. Not that he'd necessarily stop seeing her once the bet's deadline passed. Actually, if all went well tonight, he'd see her every day. He'd try to talk her into being the child psychologist for his clinic and maybe…eventually…even his wife.

He almost choked at the thought of proposing to someone, anyone, but Charlotte was a different breed than the usual women he'd dated. Other than her being a little secretive about her home life, he could find no major flaws.

She was bright, warm, considerate of others, fascinated by the psychology of children and an all-around lovely person. A woman like Charlotte must have attracted plenty of attention before, although she *was* only twenty-two. Men at that age sometimes overlooked the gems before their eyes. He wouldn't make their mistake.

"Over here," he called as he stepped into her line of sight. She got out of the car and walked toward him, the dwindling light behind her giving her hair a halo effect.

She nibbled on her lower lip. "Am I late?" She checked her uncomplicated brown-strap wristwatch. "Does the film start at seven or seven-thirty?"

"Seven-thirty, so relax. We've got time to load up on popcorn and everything." He took her hand in his. He pressed gently against her baby-soft skin, the rapid pulse like the flutter of a hummingbird's wings underneath. She smiled up at him and his heart paused mid-beat.

"So, a romantic comedy," she said. "Interesting choice, Will. Can I ask a question?"

He laughed. "Can I stop you?"

She smiled again. "Guess not. I was just wondering, did you choose this movie with me *specifically* in mind, because you thought I *personally* would love to see two people having a romantic misadventure in Athens, or because you figured this was the kind of film women stereotypically liked?"

"Neither."

Her eyebrows shot up. "You're kidding."

"Nope. It reminded me a little of *Roman Holiday*, probably my favorite classic film. I hoped you'd like a movie in that style also. Why? Would you rather see something else?"

"No, but…" She squinted at him, and he could tell she wasn't buying it. She let go of his hand, and he felt a stab of disappointment.

"But nothing. It's true. Nobody was cooler than Gregory Peck," he said, stuffing his fists in his pockets. "I don't know about the actor in this flick, but if he's half as good, it'll be worth it."

"You'd seriously choose a modern romance over some macho action-adventure film?"

Why did she look so shocked? Couldn't a guy enjoy a bantering, humorous love story without suspicion? "Yes, in this case, I would," he said.

"Hmm." She laced her fingers together and concentrated on something he couldn't see on the sidewalk in front of her. "But you like sports. And camping. And very masculine things."

"What are you afraid of, Charlotte? Think I'm a wimp because I'd sometimes rather see a guy fight back with his wit than with a weapon?"

"No, just surprised, I guess. You hadn't mentioned liking romantic comedies in your Love Match profile."

He rolled his eyes. "Oh, that. Well, shoot me now if you're gonna hold versatility against me, sweetheart. I'm a doctor. I love my work, but I also love the Cubs, my mother, good movies of any genre and dancing at weddings."

"No! Dancing? At *weddings?*" Now she looked horrified, but there was a tiny quirk in the corners of her lips that gave her away. "I'll only believe *that* when I see it."

He stopped and grinned at her. "Stick around long enough, Charlotte, and just maybe you will."

She seemed to shiver beside him, a flash of disbelief—or was it worry?—in her eyes. He wrapped his arm around her shoulders to warm her up then led her into the movie theater lobby. He liked Charlotte. He wasn't going to let her pull away from him so easily this time.

And he vowed right then and there that, despite his less-than-sincere Love Match motives, he'd prove his worthiness to her. Because he wanted her to like him back. A whole lot.

***

It was as though a dam had broken between them, Beth thought. She didn't understand it, but they couldn't stop holding hands. Or hugging. Or giving each other light kisses. Or smiling at each other like teenagers on their first date.

As they sat in the back row of the movie theater, the lights dimming and the previews rolling, Will whispered, "Popcorn?" He rubbed a buttery nugget along her bottom lip, which left a tantalizing, salty trail.

"Mmm." She opened her mouth and crunched. His fingers stayed clear of her teeth but didn't leave her face. He gently ran his thumb along the length of her jaw before planting feathery kiss on her cheek. She giggled. He laughed in response.

An older lady in the row ahead of them turned around and said, "Shhh. The movie's starting."

They broke apart. The popcorn tub tipped and buttery kernels scattered all over them.

"Oops, sorry," Will said, but the twinkle in his eye told her he wasn't the least bit repentant.

The opening credits to the movie started, but Beth couldn't concentrate on the screen. Her heart drummed as if keeping time with a jungle beat. What had happened to her ability to distance herself emotionally from this man? Where was her logic? She was supposed to be *studying* him, for goodness sake, not falling in love with him.

The characters on the screen proved to be of little interest to her for the first half hour. Who cared what "Quentin and Irene" were saying when Will's breath flowed so close to her ear? When his gentle fingers warmed hers? But, finally, one of their voices broke through Beth's haze.

"It was a complicated story!" Irene, the film's heroine, cried, posing with the Parthenon behind her silky blond head and looking distraught. Beth refocused her eyes and stared up at the woman's larger-than-life image. Irene gasped for air and let a well-rehearsed tear flow down her cheek. *"I'm sorry, Quentin, but I didn't know how to explain what happened back in Boston."*

Quentin, the equally monolithic hero, paused before sweeping his hand across the screen to indicate the sprawl of modern-day Athens below them. *"So you chose to hide the truth from me? Waiting until we were in this Old World city to admit to me your New World lies?"* he said with his best method-actor sneer. *"You didn't trust me with who you really were. Now, Irene, I don't trust you."* Beth's heart skipped a beat, wondering what would happen next, recognizing all the parallels.

The movie-star hero stormed off, and Beth stole a sideways glance at Will. He was nodding. She tensed and Will caught her gaze.

"Don't worry," he said with a grin, softly squeezing her hand. "I have every confidence that they'll get back together within the next hour."

She gave him a thin smile. If only real life could be as predictable. An hour later, with the film's happy couple safely on their Aegean Sea honeymoon cruise, Beth and Will strolled out of the cinema and onto the suburban-neighborhood sidewalk.

"Did you like it?" he asked, still holding her hand.

"Uh…yeah. Definitely. It was great. How about you?"

"I'd give it a thumbs up."

She took a deep breath. "So, Will, I have a question."

He looked heavenward and cringed. "Should I be worried?"

"Well, maybe, but—"

He laughed. "Just ask it."

"Okay. You know how Irene and Quentin had their one big argument up on the Acropolis? When he accused her of lying to him?"

"Yeah. Only he didn't just *accuse* her. She *did* lie."

"Well, right," she said. "She had her reasons, but she obviously lied. Quentin forgave her, though. He didn't hold her lie against her permanently. If you were him, would you have been able to overlook a bad start like that, given the way Irene truly cared about him, or would you have thought, as his best friend did, that Quentin should ditch her?"

"If it were real life and not a romantic comedy?" he said.

She nodded, her pulse galloping.

Will inhaled slowly and seemed to hold his breath. Then the air whooshed out of him like a gust of Arctic wind. "Hard to say," he said. "I mean, we've all lied about something, sometime. And I guess we can usually think of ways to justify the lies."

He shot her an odd look, and Beth squirmed in her sneakers. Did he suspect the depth of her dishonesty?

"But some lies people tell are worse than others," he added. "No doubt about it. If a person is protecting someone or trying to achieve a greater good like Irene was doing, the lie might still be wrong, but it's not *as* wrong—I don't think—as if someone lied about his or her essential self. That's the kind of lie Quentin thought Irene was telling at first, so his reaction in breaking things off was realistic. At least until he learned the truth. Uh, why do you ask?"

"Oh, just curious." She studied the cracks in the pavement, the new buds on the bushes next to them, the brick on the building walls. "So, you believe there are *levels* to lies?"

"Yeah, don't you?"

She shook her head. "No, not really. Because that implies we have the power to decide what's a good lie and what's a bad one. That we can then appoint ourselves as judge. It's dangerous."

Another odd expression crossed Will's face. "So, you're saying the penalty for lying should be the same, whether a person is telling a white lie or a whopper?" He raised his palms. "Fibbing to save someone's feelings or to help a larger cause is pretty different from lying for less honorable reasons."

"The situations are different, Will, and the consequences are likely to be much more severe with the whopper than with the fib, but a lie is still not the truth. Degrees don't exist. Just like someone can't be a little pregnant. Either you are or you're not. Either you lied or you didn't. But the question I asked was whether or not you'd *forgive* Irene. You're saying that because she lied for a higher goal, you probably would, right?"

"Right. But what? You don't think I should? You think I should've held it against her?"

"No," she said. "I think you, or Quentin really, should have forgiven her regardless, without waiting for proof later, because that's what love is. He claimed to love her, didn't he? He knew she loved him and wouldn't purposely hurt him. It wasn't her *love* of him that he questioned. It was his lack of knowledge about something outside of them."

Will stopped and stared at her. "But it was also about trust, Charlotte. How could he trust her if she'd kept the whole story a secret for so long? You either trust someone or you don't."

"So you believe there are degrees of truth but not degrees of trust? That's inconsistent. It's like saying some lies inspire trust while others don't. Lies do not inspire trust, period. But if you trust someone, you're trusting in how that person perceives the world, which may or may not be *your* way. You're trusting in the other person's vision of truth, and trusting her reasons for lying or for withholding information, even if those reasons don't match yours."

"Remind me not to get into a theoretical argument

with you." He leaned down and kissed her forehead. "I can't believe I'm saying this, because men are supposed to be more logical than emotional, but trust for me comes down to instinct. To intuition. I can usually feel it in my gut if I trust someone or not." He gave her a sincere look. "And though I don't know about Quentin and Irene, I do know that I trust you."

She swallowed then faked a smile. Oh, boy. She either had to tell him the truth about her real life right *now* or, to be fair to him, she had to end their relationship.

Only she didn't want it to end. There was too much about Will she'd quickly grown to like and respect. He was a man she could easily see loving, but only if no lies hovered between them.

Perhaps if she started with one thing, a small thing like her age, maybe. "Um, Will—"

"Lydia! How are you?" he said.

Who? Beth turned to see a cute young woman coming toward them and waving. She walked with a sway to her hips and brushed her hair back with an alluring swish. Beth's anxiety shot up.

"Dr. Darcy, hi!" the lady called. But as she moved closer Beth realized this Lydia of Will's was no woman. She was barely past girlhood. In fact, she looked like a teenager.

Beth squinted between the two of them and tried to discern their relationship. She felt an unfamiliar rush of jealousy when Lydia bear-hugged Will. Who was this person?

"Charlotte, I'd like you to meet one of my favorite patients. Lydia Jenkins, this is Charlotte Lucas."

"Hi, Charlotte," Lydia said, pumping Beth's hand enthusiastically.

Beth relaxed a notch. "Nice to meet you, Lydia."

Will put a hand on Lydia's shoulder. "How's Brittany doing?"

"Oh, Doc, that's what I'm so happy about. The antibiotics you gave her helped right quick. I'm fine, too." The girl beamed a look of idol-worship at him.

"Glad to hear it, darling. But I want you two to swing by this week for a checkup. I need to give your lungs a listen." The girl looked panicked at his words. Will responded accordingly. "This'll be for five minutes, Lydia, on my lunch hour, okay. No forms, no charge, no insurance. I just need to check my work, make sure I did a good job. Could you help me out with that?"

"Well, 'course I can, Doc." She bobbed her head a few times. "I—I, um, just really wanted to thank you for, you know, before."

"Thank me by getting yourself and Brittany in to see me on Tuesday. How does twelve-thirty sound?"

Lydia smiled. "Okay. See ya then." Then she bounced away.

Will's gaze followed the girl as she left, and Beth's heart swelled with admiration for the man. He was a doctor who genuinely cared about his patients. It wasn't a mere job where he could display his prestige for the wealth-conscious eyes of the world. No. Will Darcy was born to practice medicine in the trenches and to fight for those unable to go to battle themselves.

"You seem to have really been there when she needed you," Beth said, trying not to overpower him with her own idolization.

He put his arm around her shoulders and squeezed. "Lydia had her daughter last year, a few days after she turned nineteen. The two of them came down with pneumonia recently and all I did was get to it before it got worse. But dealing with an infant, no family around to help, not much money and a health crisis is tough. Too tough, I think, for someone so young. I wish I could have helped her more."

A niggling of something unsettling landed on Beth's spine. She tried to shake it off, but couldn't quite manage it.

"Though, you know," Will continued with a speculative gleam in his eye, "you could be of great help also. Like I told you when we first met, you'd make a wonderful addition to our team. The clinic will be underway late this summer, and we'll need a child psychologist. You'd be able to work closely with us while still furthering your studies in graduate school if you wanted." He tossed her one of his winning smiles.

She tried to hide her cringe. "You've already begun assembling a team?"

"Oh, yeah. Not everyone's been hired on yet, but a good group of people are interested. I've got a great dietitian-nutritionist who wants to work with us part time, a pharmacist, a psychiatrist, several physicians on staff and even a lead on a social worker."

"A social worker? Really?"

"Yes, well, it was a necessity. And the guy's just on the fringe of the project. A consultant. Your role would be much bigger and more important." He held her hand and turned her to face him. His stance was like a man proposing marriage, not like one offering a job. "Just think of the work you could do. The benefit to the community and to the individuals within it. Think how much these women would appreciate your helpfulness and insights into their children's psychological worlds."

These women. That was what he'd said, right?

And that was when she realized she'd misread the truth behind Will's wistful expression when he'd gazed at

Lydia. It wasn't just dedication to his patients, although that was a part of it. Nor was it just empathy for someone experiencing what his mom had.

It was also pity. *Pity.*

He felt sorry for Lydia, for her life, for the choices she'd made and the consequences she had to live with. And if he'd met *Beth*—not Charlotte—he'd pity her, too. Perhaps he'd want to help her, maybe even rescue her, but would he ever *see* her? Think of her as someone other than another needy patient? Would he be capable of knowing her? Of completely loving her?

She doubted it.

Whether or not she felt she had enough information to do her sociology paper justice, it would just have to do.

Whether or not his kisses touched her heart, she'd just have to learn to live without them again.

Whether or not Will could have been her "Perfect Match" was irrelevant now.

Both of them would have to move on and seek their soul mates elsewhere—with or without "Lady Catherine's" help.

He walked her back to her car and pulled her into his arms. She gave him one chaste peck on the cheek.

He tried to entice her to go out for coffee or dessert somewhere. She politely declined.

He attempted to pin down a time and a place for their next date. She said she'd have to check her schedule.

He promised to email her tomorrow. She didn't make any promises.

"Goodnight, Charlotte," he said, stepping back as she swung the car door closed.

"Thank you, Will," she replied, letting herself smile longingly at him one last time. "Goodbye."

CHAPTER SEVEN

Will stared at the computer screen, scanning the unread messages for the third time. Charlotte's name appeared nowhere on the list. He'd emailed her twice already in the past few days, but he'd gotten no response. Was her computer down? A problem, maybe, with her server? She'd always answered promptly in the past, but he had a bad feeling about it this time. There was a finality in their last parting that he didn't like.

"Cuz, how are you?"

Bingley's enthused voice grated against Will's nerves. He gritted his teeth before swiveling his chair to face his cousin. "Fine. And you?"

"Absolutely outstanding. Just golfed eighteen record-breaking holes with my pals at the club. Stock market's climbing steadily this week. Met a pretty manicurist named Scarlet, if you can believe it, at—"

"I can believe it. Glad to hear things are going so well for you." He shuffled a few medical charts around to simulate that 'busy doctor' look. Bingley, as always, ignored the hint.

His cousin gave the office his usual once-over before zoning in on the one item Will wished he'd thought to put away. "Hey, is that her? The Love-Match Lady?" Bingley picked up the first of the Polaroid snapshots. The one of Will and Charlotte at his mother's house. His cousin eyed it up, down and sideways. "Nice choice, Cuz. She's cute. Very, very cute. So—" he turned his attention back to Will, "when's the wedding?"

Will forced himself not to roll his eyes. "No date's been set. Now listen, Bingley—"

"Have you asked her yet or not? Remember, double the money if you get her to wear a ring."

"I remember and, no, of course not. We've only been on four dates. I still need to take her on a fifth to fulfill that first part of our bargain, and even then I doubt I should be bringing up marriage. Our last evening out ended kind of…oddly. She hasn't answered my emails this week, so I don't know what's up with her. She told me she didn't have a cell. Never revealed where she worked. The university won't give out information on students. And her name's not listed in the white pages, so I can't call her at home. Okay? Now can we just drop it?"

Bingley stared at him with his irritating know-it-all look. "The five dates were part of our bargain…yes," he murmured. "But what about the other part? The little get-together where I meet her on or before my birthday? I still need to get a look at this woman in the flesh, you know. Gotta talk to her and make sure you haven't connived her into striking some kind of deal with you on the side. Maybe she's the kind that'll do anything for a quick buck."

Something in Will's head exploded. "Bingley, get out! No matter what you say, I know you don't have my 'best interests' at heart. Isn't it enough that I'm playing your childish little game, jumping through your stupid hoops in order to raise funding for the clinic? Isn't it enough for you to see me wriggling around on your money-baited hook, feeling like a fool for letting you manipulate me? Do you have to insult *her*, too?"

Bingley's brows rose. "Why, Cuz, I do believe this is the first time in over thirty years you've been more concerned with a woman's reputation than with your god-awful ambition to seek revenge on the system." He paused and tilted his chin upward before narrowing his eyes to green slits. "I think, for all your whining, you might be dangerously close to fulfilling my bargain after all." He dropped the snapshot on the desk, turned neatly on his heel and marched out.

Will picked up the first clipboard within his reach and flung it across the room. It smashed into the wall with a satisfying thud, but he still felt crummy. Then he turned back to the computer and began to compose yet another email to Charlotte Lucas.

***

Beth checked her computer for emails three minutes before the end of the day. She read Will's latest message with both curiosity and a powerful jab of guilt:

Hi there, Charlotte.

Me again. Didn't know if my previous messages hadn't reached you or if you've just been too busy to reply. Hoped to see you again this weekend, if possible, or even during the workweek if that's the only time you're available. We could grab lunch or a quick cup of coffee. There's a nutty flavor at the Koffee Haus that I want to taste again—Macadamia Hawaiian Kona. Tempted? You've got all my numbers—cell, home, work—so give me a call or a quick email and let me know. I miss talking to you. Take care of yourself.

Will

Beth's fingers itched to reply.

Her heart tightened at the thought of letting him down. But it had to be. There was no future for the two of them, and she'd rather he thought she was a fickle young woman who didn't know a good man when she saw one rather than a lying single mother-slash-social worker who knew she could never live up to his expectations.

From her one and only work drawer, she pulled out the snapshot of the two of them. She could almost re-experience the delight she'd felt at the moment at his mother's house when Will's arm hugged her shoulders and he leaned in toward her. Her pulse did a cha-cha at the thought. For a few joyous seconds that day, she'd come close to believing fairy tales could come true. That rich, handsome doctors could really fall in love with practically penniless single moms struggling to stay off welfare.

Beth switched off the computer yet again without responding to Will, and she headed home for the day.

Jane tapped her foot by the apartment door in typical impatience as Beth and Charlie approached. She held up a large brown paper bag with Chinese letters scrawled all over the side. "Dinner," her friend announced. "Now let me in. I've been waiting a whole six minutes for you two slowpokes."

"Egg rolls?" Charlie asked eagerly, tripping a little on the carpet before giving Jane a hard welcoming squeeze.

"Yep." Jane puffed out some air. "Boy, kid, you sure got some muscles on you."

He giggled. Beth unlocked the door and they all fell into the room. Within minutes they were munching on egg rolls and seafood cow-chow-tay. Beth eyed her friend showing off her expertise with chopsticks. Then a scallop slipped out of Jane's tenuous grasp, and she used one of the wooden sticks to spear it. White sauce splattered on her jersey.

"Oh, don't give me that disapproving look, Beth Ann Bennet. You're just jealous because I can use these objects of torture—not very well, I'll admit—while you won't even take a chance on it." She swiped at her white-speckled shirt with a House of China napkin. "Why not trade in your fork for a set of chopsticks, for once? Why are you so afraid of taking risks?"

Beth felt she could live without this discussion tonight. Her elderly client Lynn Hammond had urged her to take a risk and look what happened. "I'm not *afraid*, Jane. I just—well, I—"

"Cut the garbage. This is *me*, your best friend, remember? What's fueling all this fear of yours, and you know darned well I'm not talking about eating utensils?"

"You know the reasons." She stabbed her final piece of shrimp with her fork and scooped up the last of the fried rice. Her son, his attention fixed on their small TV set, chomped on his second egg roll and ignored them in favor of Winnie the Pooh.

"Not specific enough, Beth. Spell it out for me."

She shot a pointed look in her son's direction and then returned her gaze to Jane. "Now's not the right time."

Jane sighed. "It's never the right time." But she held her tongue until Charlie was out of the room. "C'mon, Beth. Something's going on with you. You're practically pulsing with anxiety. Is there a problem at work? Something happening with school? Or Charlie? What?"

Beth knew she couldn't hold back the truth now. She told Jane about her latest dates with Will, the ones she'd kept secret. "I intended to break it off, that was always my plan, but there's so much about him that just, oh…touches me, I guess. I tried to stop seeing him, but until this week I didn't succeed. I told myself it wasn't fair to write about him or to do the project without his full story—"

"You met his *mother*, for heaven's sake. You ought to have enough background research for a three-hundred-page dissertation by now."

"Well, yes. I know. But as for my own curiosity and interest in him…"

"Don't go there, Beth. It's dangerous. I know I've kidded you about taking risks, and I think opening your heart up to someone new is a great idea in most circumstances, but not with the way things are lined up here. You went too far and too long with the Charlotte Lucas lie. Maybe if you'd told him right away—after that first date—your relationship might've gotten straightened out enough to go forward, but—"

"No. He didn't know me well enough then. He wouldn't have given me a chance if he'd found out so soon. Think about it, Jane. He hated my profession. He didn't want to get involved with a woman who had a child. He *did* want someone he thought might jump into this clinic thing with him. I failed all three of his primary hopes and expectations, and he doesn't even know it. Besides, back then everything we discussed or knew about each other was surface stuff—"

"Your profiles."

"Right. We were cardboard characters to one another. That wasn't the kind of knowledge that would inspire someone to stick around through even normal challenges. Now that our relationship is deeper, more intimate, my lie is more like a betrayal than ever." She told Jane about Will's recent emails.

"So, you're just avoiding the guy? I don't know, Beth.

What happens if you run into him somewhere? If he finds out the truth from someone other than you?"

Beth laughed humorlessly. "From whom? Will and I don't run in the same circles. At all. And we live in Chicago, not some tiny country village. With a few million people and several socioeconomic levels between us, I doubt our paths will ever cross again."

She tossed her plastic dinner plate into the sink none too gently. It wasn't as though she had to worry about chipping her rose-patterned china, now did she? Her head hurt and the rest of her ached with regret. "Besides, I care about him, Jane. Despite our differences. I don't want to hurt him, and I can't keep deceiving him. This might not be the only way but, in the end, I think it'll be the kindest."

"If you say so," Jane said, cracking open a fortune cookie. She handed another one to Beth. "Here."

Beth took the unopened cookie, but she knew her fortune already. It could only say: "Expect hard work, years of struggle and much loneliness." She just hoped all her sacrifices would pay off so Charlie could someday have the fortune she most wished for him. The one that read: "You will have a happy and fulfilling life."

***

Will didn't know what had come over him. He stared through the glass of the store window and wanted to bang his head against it. It would serve him right.

He was behaving like a fool, his conduct the most irrational and illogical known to mankind. The goals and ambitions typically heading his list of critical To Do's had dwindled from community-based humanitarian and altruistic objectives to personal and strikingly selfish ones.

He wanted to marry Charlotte Lucas. And here was the big twist: It wasn't because of Bingley's bet. He wanted to shove Bingley's idiotic bet in a place his cousin would be hard pressed to find it. He wanted to come clean with Charlotte about his reasons for seeking someone on the Lady Catherine website and explain how quickly his motives for spending time with her had changed. He wanted to talk with her for hours, hold her in his arms, kiss her, make her his wife. There seemed to be no end to the things he wanted.

Man, what was wrong with him? It was preposterous to feel so strongly about a woman he'd only gone on four dates with. A woman who hadn't contacted him for nine long days, so he had no idea if there'd be a fifth date or not.

He wasn't the kind of guy to shake his fists at the gods and insist upon a just and moral universe. He knew—and, boy, did he ever—that life wasn't fair. That good people sometimes got dealt a bad hand and bad people sometimes got away with murder or at least the occasional fender-bender. It was pointless to pretend otherwise.

But Charlotte blowing him off? That was so damned unfair.

And not just because he'd lose out on a wonderful and warm child psychologist at the clinic. No. It was her. He really liked *her*. The very woman she was. Her smile, her attitude, her laughter. The way her wild hair blew in the wind. The gazillion questions she asked.

He groaned. He was falling in love with someone who had all the natural charm and good looks he'd vowed not to seek in a life partner. She possessed every clichéd trait a man like him was drawn to—none of which was the basis for a successful, long-lasting relationship.

Not that he cared.

She could've been anything…a waitress, a dog-walker,

a romance writer, whatever. For the first time in his life, he realized it didn't matter.

But, thankfully, even that was perfect. Only one problem. She held every hand in the deck. If she didn't want to reach him, she wouldn't have to. Even if he snuck an ace up his sleeve—like that princess-cut engagement ring winking at him from the jeweler's window—it wouldn't matter one iota if the dealer didn't give him a chance to play.

He took one last look at the row of rings and wedding bands before he walked away.

***

"Mommy, why do we have to go back into your work?" Charlie said, squeezing a mud-stained baseball in his little fist. "I thought we were going to the park now. I wanna play ball. Do you know how to pitch? Mikey says I'm not so good at it and that I need to practice. Do you think I need to practice? Is it easier to pitch or catch? Mikey says it's—"

"Charlie, darling?"

"Yeah?"

"I know you want to play catch at the park so—"

"And pitch, too."

"Right. And pitch, too. But I need to pick up a folder at the office so I can do my work later. If I wait too long, the afternoon will be over and the doors will be locked. And since I don't have a key…"

"Okay, Mommy. We can go there first."

"Thank you, Charlie."

Beth sighed and parked her car in the Social Services lot. She hadn't told Charlie this yet, but they'd also need to stop for gas. She'd been running on fumes and hope for the last two days. She checked her wallet, praying she'd have enough for a quarter of a tank. With the couple dollars she found, they might just manage to make it through the week.

"Come with me, sweetie," she told her son. "I don't want you staying alone in the car."

"Will Robby be in there today?"

"Oh, I think so. Abby, too, I'll bet."

"Alrighty! She lets me have lollipops from her candy jar."

Beth grinned. "Yes, she does. But remember, don't pester her. And you may only have one lollipop if she offers it to you first. Understand?"

He grimaced. "Uh-huh."

"Good."

They reached the office and Charlie was immediately spirited away by a high-fiving, back-slapping, arm-wrestling Robby, who was the proud father of three daughters, none of whom enjoyed roughhousing.

She dug through the mass of paperwork in search of Anna Marie Dermott's file. After a four-minute hunt, she found it. The elderly lady was on her list of visits tomorrow, and she wanted to be prepared.

"Hey, Beth, what brings you back again?" Dan asked, stepping out of his office and sending a smile and a wave her way.

She held up the file. "Nothing major. I just wanted to grab this so I could look over the latest additions to it tonight."

"Ah," her boss said. "Being conscientious as always, I see."

She answered his compliment the only way she could, with a small grin. Besides, what could anyone say to something like that without sounding prideful?

Dan patted her shoulder in his usual fatherly manner. "Keep up the great work, kiddo." He checked his watch and shook his head. "My four-thirty appointment's late." He shot her a commiserating glance as if to say, *Can you believe some people?*

She laughed and nodded. Dan strode back into his office.

She heard Charlie giggling in the other room and Abby's voice saying to him in an extra-loud stage whisper, "Hey, slugger, want a lollipop? Cherry or grape? Or, if you don't tell your mom, you can have both." Charlie agreed to the deal mighty quick.

Beth couldn't bring herself to break in on him too soon. Much as her little boy loved the park, he loved the attention he got from caring adults most of all. She wished there were even more in his life, but she sure wouldn't complain. She had some great people surrounding and supporting her. Anybody who cared about her, cared about Charlie, too.

And she wouldn't have it any other way. It was the main reason, she told herself for the eight hundredth time, why things with Will would never work...even if every one of their other differences could be magically resolved. There was simply no getting around the fact that he'd never want to be a stepfather.

She picked up the framed photo of Charlie on her desk. It was taken at school only a few months ago but already it looked out of date. His hair had lightened a tad from playing in the spring sunshine. It would get nearly as blond as Pete's by the end of summer.

Genetics. So strange.

Fortunately, Charlie's and Pete's personalities differed more than their hair did. For starters, she'd taught her son manners and responsibility.

She checked her watch. Four-forty, and Charlie was still playing some incomprehensible game with Robby

involving a tin garbage can and paperclips. It was okay.
The days stayed lighter longer now and dinner wouldn't
be anything to rush home for anyway. There was plenty
of time.

She heard footsteps and a shuffling of papers outside
the office door. Another delighted screech from Charlie.
Abby talking in her usual animated tone on the telephone.
Beth was straightening the files on her desk when the
door swung open.

She didn't bother looking up at first, but a haunting
silence pierced the office atmosphere. It seemed directed
at her. She glanced toward the door at the same moment
as a familiar voice rang out.

"Charlotte?" Will said. "Is that you?"

CHAPTER EIGHT

Beth stared at him. She couldn't blink. She couldn't open her mouth. She couldn't breathe. Will's expression stole her speech. His face was etched with warring emotions—delight, surprise, a flicker of hurt.

A heartbeat later Charlie rushed out of the room, Robby at his heels. Her son bounded over to her desk, one lollipop in his hand and one in his mouth. "Mommy, look what Abby gave me," he said, his words garbled. He slurped loudly on the cherry pop and waved the unopened grape treat at her.

Her head turned in Charlie's direction, only slightly, but it was enough. She caught a few new emotions flitting across Will's face—shock, disbelief, comprehension, anger. All followed by a powerful wave of betrayal, which washed all the others away, she thought, at least temporarily.

"Charlotte?" The name came out of him liked a choked whisper.

"Who's Charlotte?" Robby asked at the same moment that Dan swung his office door open.

"Hey, Doc," Dan declared. "Glad you were able to make it."

"My apologies for being late, Mr. Noelen. We had victims from a five-car pile-up come in the ER this afternoon." As Will spoke, his clear blue eyes speared her like icy needles.

Abby, being drawn to the room by new voices, regarded the doctor with growing curiosity. Beth caught the inquisitive social worker shooting perplexed glances between her and Will, and she knew Abby would figure out the relationship between them faster than a teen heartbreak.

Beth stood up. "I—I should go," she announced to no one in particular.

Dan put a light hand on her shoulder. "Well, before you do, let me introduce you guys to Dr. Will Darcy, attending ER physician at Regents General Hospital."

"Will?" Abby whispered, her eyes quizzical. Beth could almost see the woman's brain synapses making connections.

"Yes," Dan said. "We're trying to work out a way to help him on a new clinic he's starting up for low-income mothers and their children." He turned toward Abby. "This is Abby Kraigenmeier, Doc. She's one of our five senior social workers and has been with us for—what? Ten years now?"

"Eleven in September," Abby said proudly. She waved at Will. "Nice to meet you, Dr. Darcy."

Will sent Abby a sincere-looking but somewhat weak smile.

"And this is Robby Benjamin, also a senior social worker," Dan said. "At the agency for seven years."

Robby reached out to shake Will's hand. "Nice meetin' you."

Will nodded. "You, too, thanks." His eyes strayed back to Beth. Dan glanced between them, looking more puzzled than Beth had ever seen him.

"The newest member of our team," Dan said, "is Beth Bennet. She's been one of our social work assistants this past year. We're hoping she'll be able to join us full time next month."

Will stared at her. "Beth, is it?" he said.

She swallowed before nodding slowly. A flash of anger returned to his eyes but, before either of them could say anything more, Dan continued. "And this little firecracker," Dan ruffled the top of Charlie's head, "is Beth's son Charlie."

"I'm six," Charlie proclaimed, sticking out his hand for Will to shake.

Will reached for it, gently grasping her little boy's palm. "Six years old, huh?" He paused, holding Charlie's gaze for a long moment. "That's pretty big." Will looked at Beth again, for the first time his expression unreadable. Then he glanced at Dan. "I brought my proposal, as you asked. Perhaps we should get started."

"Sure thing, Doc. My office is over here. Go on in. I'll be there in a second." Dan ushered Will out of the room, the doctor's jaw tight and his eyes fixed on Dan's office door. Dan then turned back and gave Beth a strange look. "You okay, kiddo?" he whispered. "Is something going on that I should know about?"

Beth didn't move for several seconds.

Abby snapped her fingers in front of Beth's face. "Is this 'Will,' by chance, the *same* 'Will' you were talking to Jane about on the phone that one day?"

Beth glanced between Abby and Dan. Her boss crossed his arms and gave her an expectant look.

"Oh, brother," Abby muttered.

Robby leaned in. "And, uh, Beth? Why'd the doc call you Charlotte?"

Beth squeezed her eyes shut, grabbed Charlie's hand and pulled herself and her son out of there.

***

The phone stopped ringing after five and a half hours. Beth couldn't bring herself to answer and, since she just had an old plastic wall phone without Caller ID and she didn't waste money on extras like voicemail, she didn't know for sure who'd been calling.

She had her guesses, of course.

Dan, Abby, Robby, Jane, maybe even Will, if he'd pounded his fist on Dan's desk and demanded her number. She could almost imagine him talking to her boss after she'd left: "What is Charlotte's, I mean, *Beth's* phone number? I need to have a few words with her about how she lied to me and pretended to be the kind of woman I'd actually date."

To which Dan would reply: "I can't believe I put my trust in her. This colors my opinion of her as a social worker, and there's no way I could, in good conscience, recommend her for the full-time position now."

Both men would nod in agreement, and Beth would have lost everything she'd spent all these years sacrificing for. And, worst of all, Charlie would lose out, too.

Her son had gone to bed exhausted an hour ago. "Why didn't we get to play at the park?" he'd asked, but only once. She figured the look on her face had probably frightened him into silence. Instead, he'd gotten macaroni and cheese for dinner, a whole ninety-minute Disney video and splash time in his bath until his fingertips turned pruney. She, in return, got to cry uninterrupted in her bedroom for most of the night—alone time punctuated only by the shrill ring of the telephone.

Of course, even without the incessant ringing, she couldn't sleep. So, instead, she stayed up and wrote and wrote…and typed and typed. And lied…and lied some more because what would a research paper be with only facts? Wasn't this what was called "creative nonfiction"?

Well, not creative enough because her words on the page were still too close to the truth. She couldn't seem to figure a way to distance herself from the project. She remembered her night with Will at the movies. The way he'd kissed her. The way her hands were warmed by his and her heart set aflame. Their intellectual debate on trust and the passion with which he declared his trust in her. How could she describe the truth of her admiration for him, whatever their gender differences might be?

She couldn't, so she wrote, "Case Study #1 values both intuition and logic, which contrasts with the stereotype that men consistently put their confidence in the rational over the emotional."

Yes, it was a fact. No, it wasn't the truth. Not the real truth of her soul. But then, Professor O'Reilly didn't want to read about how she was falling in love with a man who surely despised her. It was going to have to be enough to just finish the darned paper…and to do it without acting on the urge to rip every single page to shreds.

Morning came with the rising sun—a usual occurrence in most of the world, but today Beth felt a shiver of surprise. Life really did go on no matter what, didn't it?

Bleary-eyed and achy, she got Charlie off to school and, for the first time in months, called in sick to the agency. Her heart pounded as she spoke with the cheerful receptionist. Beth said she was feeling terrible. (True.) She said she had an awful headache. (Also true.) She said she didn't sleep a wink last night. (True again.) When asked if she knew what kind of illness she had—bad virus, common cold, the flu—she said she wasn't sure. (Bald-faced lie.)

She knew all the symptoms of heart sickness, and she had them in spades.

Just as she was about to hang up, the kindly woman's words became muffled on the other end of the line as though some agency debate raged around the lady.

"Beth?" the receptionist said. "Dan overheard me talking with you. He wanted to ask you something. Can you hold the line while I transfer your call to his office?" She didn't give Beth a chance to answer, but what could she say? *No, I've been dreading this conversation with Dan, and I'm not going to have it with him…*

Yeah, right.

"Okay, dearie. Hope you feel better," the woman said before redirecting the line.

A split-second later Dan's voice came on. "Beth, how are you feeling?"

She waited a few heartbeats, expecting more. Expecting his negative judgment of her. "Not great," she admitted finally. "I can get some paperwork done at home, though. And, if you still want me to, I can be in the office first thing tomorrow. I still need to see Mrs. Dermott and go through—"

"No, that's not a good idea. Robby had a cancellation. He can run over there today. I want you to take a few days off."

She *knew* it. That was it for her at Social Services. In a few days, after he'd had a chance to regroup and gather candidates for Mimi's position, Dan would call her into his office and demand that she leave for good. Oh, brother. Would she even pass her field practicum now? She had to know. "Dan, I—I'm sorry if yesterday was awkward for you. I hadn't expected Will to have any connection with the agency or I never would've—"

"Beth, kiddo, I want to talk about this. I think we *need* to talk about it. But not today. Your relationship with Dr. Darcy isn't really my concern. I asked him a few questions, by the way, and he was as chatty as a mime when it came to you. He talked full speed for an hour about his clinic but the only thing he said about you was your name, Beth Bennet, like it was a big mystery…which, I gather, it was."

From Beth's side of the phone line she could've sworn Dan was holding back laughter. "So, you'll let me finish my field work?" she said.

"Of course."

She nearly collapsed on the carpet with relief. "And Mimi's position? Are you still willing to recommend me for it?" She clutched the receiver until her knuckles throbbed.

"I'm still willing to recommend you, Beth, but my question is whether or not you really want to do it."

"But I do! Naturally, I want—"

"Oh, I know," Dan said. "I know you'd like a full-time job, that you have respect for social workers, that the salary increase will help you and Charlie, that you're responsible, considerate of others, conscientious. But would you be proud of your profession? And proud of yourself? Above all, would you be happy to be 'Beth Bennet' in a life that—except for a little more money—is not very different from the life you have now? That's what I wonder, Beth."

Her blood started pulsing wildly from her capillaries to her arteries. Every part of her body, toes to waist to chin, trembled with the increased flow. She tried to get her lips to form a response, but Dan continued before she could get them to cooperate.

"A truly good social worker is someone who's able to expend energy helping others because she's confident in herself and content with her life. These are the kind of people I choose for my team. With so many clients in need, we don't have room for a lot of staff-member insecurities. So I need you to reflect a little on this. Take a few days to figure out where you stand with yourself and with the field. Okay?"

"Okay," she whispered, but she felt another corner of her world on the verge of crumbling.

***

Will slept badly or, more accurately, he didn't sleep at all. Since becoming an attending physician a couple years back, he rarely spent his nights in the ER if he could help it, but a few near fatalities came in after he'd left Dan Noelen's office and, hey, why not be honest? He couldn't stand the thought of his own company when he could, instead, be saving lives and pretending to live a useful existence.

He groaned and pushed himself off the hospital cot and into the staff washroom. He glared at his reflection. Bags under the eyes. Sallow complexion. Anemic-looking, even though his hemoglobin levels were healthy. Crusty matter clinging to his lashes. And wrinkles at the edges of his face. *Wrinkles*, for goodness sake. He looked as bad as he felt.

He splashed some hot water on himself and barged into the stream of ER chaos. It was comforting. There was no space, no time for his ego or his personal problems. No room for Charlotte Lucas or Beth Bennet or whoever the hell she was today. Not a second to spare to obsess over the lost funds for the clinic.

Cripes, she had a *kid*.

But he couldn't think about that now.

He grabbed a handful of medical charts and buried himself in patients until well past noon.

When he couldn't put off lunch any longer, he snatched a burger and a cup of their awful, no-name coffee from the cafeteria. He leaned against the window by the far wall, not wanting to bother with the confinement of a table. Looking out into the hospital's courtyard, he spotted one of the first-year med students—male, Asian, early twenties, quiet—hunched up at the foot of a tree. Will downed his lunch and went out there.

"Hey, Lang, what's up?"

The young man raised his eyes to Will's, barely controlled anguish imprinted like a rubber stamp on his face. He straightened up a notch. "Nothing, Doctor."

"What do you mean, 'nothing'? You look worse than some of the ICU patients. Has there been a death in the family?"

Lang closed his eyes. "No, Dr. Darcy. I'm just aware of a death to come. Not in my family, but upstairs, third floor. A patient I've known for two months now."

Will shrugged. "It's a daily battle here. People come in. They get released. You can only try your best to try to fix what can be fixed. Make 'em comfortable. Do what has to be done. The rest? That's up to their bodies, their attitudes, their God."

The guy looked at him. Compassion and unshed tears filled those dark eyes. "I hope I can be as detached as you someday, Doctor, but I...I don't know..."

"It'll happen for you," Will said, feeling something prickly and unlikable creep down his spine at his own words, but he couldn't take time to analyze it now. Nor did he want to. "Don't worry," he told Lang. "Your reaction is normal. Every med student is oversensitive at first. Time and experience change that."

Will strode away wondering how much time and experience had changed *him*. Did he care about patients as much as he did when first he started? Was he really as "detached" as Lang implied?

Aw, forget it. His shift ended in another hour, and he had a major piece of unfinished business to deal with. He figured by the time he got to Little Miss Beth's house, he'd work himself back to feeling as fully self-righteous as he had yesterday afternoon.

He didn't want to cloud his anger with self-doubt or logic or analysis. He couldn't. He'd deal with himself and his own stupid fantasies later. But not until after he told that woman a few things. And, by all that was good or holy, she'd better listen.

***

Beth pretended all day she wasn't home. The wall phone only rang a time or two, nothing like last night, but she ignored it. No one, of course, came to the door. Why would they? She'd worked or been in class every weekday since the dawn of time, it seemed, so no one would have expected her to be hiding out in the most obvious of places.

She watched Charlie through the window as he made the transition from the school bus to Mrs. Moratti's apartment. Uneventful as usual. Not that either of them knew about her required sabbatical. She'd tell Mrs. Moratti tomorrow in case of an emergency, but today Beth was too embarrassed and too tired to offer explanations.

She pondered Dan's questions. Was she proud of herself? Did a future life as a social worker live up to her dreams and ambitions? Too many pebbles bounced around in her head for her to see the boulders clearly. Maybe the truth on this was one of those things a woman had to come at sneakily, not attack head-on. Like a kid's perception puzzle. One of those optical illusions. She could never see the 3-D picture unless she crossed her eyes or blurred her own vision somehow.

Then again, maybe gaining perspective was simpler than that. Maybe cookies and a soap opera were all that were required.

She slit open a small bag of bite-sized chocolate chip cookies Jane had left last week, saved half of them in an airtight container for Charlie and savored each and every one of the rest.

She flipped on the television and began surfing channels for something engaging. Talk shows about two-timing women who gave birth to alien babies. Celebrity entertainment reports. The financial news hour. She laughed when she got to that one. Imagine *her* investing all of her savings. "Excuse me, Mr. Money Adviser," she'd say. "I have forty-three dollars in my checking account, but I'm sure you have several remarkable ideas for how to turn that into a fortune…"

She finally tuned in to the inevitable: her favorite childhood soap opera—*The Bad, the Brave and the Brazen*. Grant and Lexie Chandler were in the midst of rousing dispute over the custody of Baby Sven.

Grant said, *"You can't use my affair as a way to keep me from seeing Sven. He's my son, too, and I won't have my parental rights denied."*

"Yeah?" Lexie replied. *"And where was all that conviction when you were off somewhere getting cozy with Miranda? You didn't care about your son then. You're only interested in him now because of Grandfather Dino's inheritance."*

Grant gave a menacing laugh. *"Listen you greedy,*

conniving—"

"I've listened to you long enough!" She threw a crimson-colored porcelain vase at him, looking pleased when it smashed on the wall above his shoulder. Shards of pottery cascaded like a rage-red waterfall over his gray designer suit.

Beth smiled. This was fun.

"Oh, but you should listen, Lexie. You like to think of yourself as above reproach, but I know your dirty little secrets," he hissed. *"I saw you…with Victor!"*

Lexie gasped. Beth chuckled.

"Yes, that's right. I know all about your plan to forge a codicil on Grandfather Dino's will." Grant brushed the last of the shattered vase chards off his suit and stood to his full height. He looked his ex-TV-wife in the eye before taking a few slow steps forward. *"And I have ways of preventing you from ever seeing Sven again if you cross me on this."*

Lexie sneered then ran her tongue over her heavily lipsticked lips. *"You forget, Grant, that I have ways of my own. Ways I know will bring you to your knees."* She, too, took a few steps forward.

Beth leaned in toward the television set.

The soap-opera couple locked eyes then lunged at each other. Instead of striking or scratching, though, Grant and Lexie began kissing with all the passion of honeymooners in Tahiti. There was a pounding on their door, and Beth wondered who had arrived. Miranda? Victor? Was Baby Sven old enough to knock?

But the couple didn't budge from their embrace. Beth looked away from the show, realizing it was someone at her own door causing the racket.

"Beth?" the voice in the hall called. "I can hear the TV. I know you're in there. Open up. Now."

Oh, no. *Will Darcy.*

CHAPTER NINE

Will let Beth Bennet inch open the door before he marched into her living room. He thought he'd done the right thing—waiting, that is, before coming over here. He thought he'd gotten his anger in check. That, despite his feelings, he'd be able to speak coherently to the woman who'd just messed up his life. But, seeing her again, right in front of his eyes, he knew this wasn't the case. He was madder now than he'd ever been.

"What kind of game were you playing, *Beth?*" He glared at her and watched as she took a few steps backward. "I want to know exactly why you were pretending to be someone who you so clearly aren't."

"Will, I, um, please come in." She motioned him toward an old brown armchair.

He thought the fabric was very 1970s, but it was clean and had a sunny yellow and white pillow on it to brighten it up. He sat.

"Can I get you something to drink? We only have orange juice, milk and water...oh, and tea bags, so I'd could make—"

"No. I didn't come here for a tea party," he said, feeling cruel, angry and hurt all at once. "I'm only interested in one thing. The truth."

She sank into a beige sofa from the same era as the armchair. "I'm not sure there are words I could say that will explain this to you. I'm sorry, if that means anything. It was never my intention to hurt you."

"The hell it wasn't. Is your name Charlotte Lucas? Are you a child psychologist? No, on both counts, right? So then your identity lies *were* intentional." He wanted to crush something with his hands. He grabbed the yellow and white pillow and squeezed.

"What I said was that it wasn't my intention to hurt you," she whispered. "It *was* my intention to lie, I'll admit. I hadn't expected to do more than email you, or maybe meet with you once, at most. What happened between us took me by surprise, Will. By the time I realized how far into it we were, it was too awkward to explain. I figured even if I did tell you the whole story that you wouldn't be able to accept the truth. That my real life would be too shocking."

He jumped up off the chair and pointed at her. "So you decided you'd think *for* me? Choose what I should or shouldn't know?"

She sighed and slumped against the back of the sofa. "Come on. Had you known the truth—that I'm a mother, that I'm planning to be a social worker—you never would've spent time with me in the first place."

He acknowledged this with a short nod and saw the pain in her eyes. He sat back down. But, hey, he wasn't going to feel sorry for her. He may have gotten into the whole Love Match dating thing because of Bingley's bet, but he'd never, not even once, lied about himself to her.

He glanced at the TV. Some guy in a gray suit pulled

away from his onscreen woman and shouted, *"We've only just begun this battle."*

The lady, pouting but with a glint of something sinister in her green eyes, pulled Gray Suit back. In the next second she nestled herself into the crook of his neck. Pouty Lady purred, *"I'm fighting to win."* Then she covered his mouth with hers.

Will looked at Beth. "What *is* this?"

Beth gave an embarrassed shrug and clicked off the TV.

After a long, silent moment, she said, "Look, Will, I'm older than you thought. I'm twenty-six not twenty-two. After years of trying to finish my undergraduate degree, I'll be completely done this month. The Love Match profile I did in March was part of a final research project for a sociology class I'm taking—"

"A research project? My God." He tossed the pillow on the carpet and covered his eyes with palms. All he'd been to her was a freaking experiment.

"Yes. But Will—"

"Do you realize you could get into serious trouble for something like this? For falsifying personal data in a public domain? We all had to click to verify their legal agreement before signing up, remember? If the owners of the Lady Catherine site found out about what you did…I don't know. This might even be a federal offense," he said, the angriest part of him liking the fact that this, at least, had her looking worried.

Her eyes grew big and round. Her lips pressed tight. Not that he'd actually report her. He hadn't read the website's agreement all that closely, so what the hell did he know? What she'd done might not even be against the law. But maybe she wouldn't be so quick to string a man along next time under false pretenses.

She brushed a few trembling fingers over her mouth and took a deep breath. "It's up to you to do what you feel is best," she said.

"And you have nothing further to add? No other explanations for your behavior?"

"I can only offer you the truth. My real story." She stared at him as if waiting for his permission to continue.

He bobbed his head in her direction.

She swallowed. "Charlie was born six years ago. He's the only good thing that came from a marriage that had a very short past and no future. His father Pete was my college boyfriend. We married on impulse, and I got pregnant right away. His parents didn't want anything to do with us." She paused. "Pete was a year older than me and, it turned out, deathly afraid of being a father. He bolted the minute he graduated. Charlie saw him for the last time when he was two months old. Obviously, he doesn't remember."

Will thought of his own mom, his own experience, and he tightened his jaw. "What about your parents?"

"They're both retired teachers, and they live in Arizona now. They were sympathetic and they didn't disown me, but it wasn't up to them to drop everything to fix my life for me either. So I flipped burgers, worked as a waitress, then as a checkout girl at the grocery store, among other jobs. Mrs. Moratti down the hall has watched Charlie since he was a toddler at half the cost of daycare because I wash her windows when they get grimy and vacuum for her and clean the snow and ice off her car in winter—"

"Why? Where are her kids?"

"Her sons live in Boston and Sarasota. And with my parents far away, she and I do the things we can to help each other. We've become a kind of family. She reminds me a little of my Grandma Kate, who I really, really loved. In some ways, with Mrs. Moratti, I kind of feel like I have my grandmother back."

He was feeling angry again, this time at himself for getting sucked into her story, for feeling empathetic against his will. He glanced around the tidy but very sparse room. "So you chose social work as a profession because...why? It's not an occupation known for its high salaries."

She nodded. "My parents asked me that as well. They'd wanted me to study engineering or law or something more lucrative. I was a good student, well organized, too, and I wanted to make at least a modest living, but I couldn't see myself in a field I wasn't passionate about. Up until Charlie was born, I'd taken all the required general studies classes and a few electives in psychology and sociology, both of which I really liked. But then I had to drop out to make money to support us."

She fidgeted with a loose thread on the sofa. "Mimi Jeffries, the lady who just left the agency, was the social worker assigned to me at the hospital when Charlie was born. I took her business card but didn't contact her for months. When I finally did, her kindness and encouragement changed the direction of my life." She smiled up at him, the first warm, radiant smile he'd seen since he'd arrived.

"I wanted to do the helpful things for other people that she'd done for me, and I especially loved being around the elderly," Beth said. "So I started picking up one or two classes at a time to finish my degree, and I began working part time at Social Services to gain experience. It's also where I'm doing my field practicum." The smile drained from her eyes.

"Dan Noelen has been a wonderful boss for me as well a caring field-work sponsor," she said. "I hope you won't take out on him any of your negative feelings toward me. He's one of the good guys."

Pride reared its ugly head, and Will just couldn't stand the thought of her playing his emotions any longer. Yes, yes, Noelen was a good guy, he'd seen that firsthand. Okay, maybe some social workers weren't like the heartless witches he'd seen terrorizing his mother back when he was a kid and in between stepfathers…

When a check for one of the school fees bounced.

When the doctor's bills couldn't be paid on time.

When the neighbor across the street reported his mom for "neglect" because she was sewing at the tailor's shop from six a.m. to eight at night in order to put food on the table.

His heart clenched as though it were trapped in a vice. "I'll allow that your experience was different from mine," he managed to say.

"Thank you. Listen, Will, I'm really sorry we—"

"Forget it, Charlotte…I mean, Beth…whoever you are," he said in his iciest voice. "The truth is, I went out with you on a bet." There, he'd said it. Now she couldn't feel sorry for him.

Her eyes turned squinty with confusion. "A *bet?*"

"You got it. My cousin Bingley was going to pour major funding into the clinic if I dated some woman five times and brought her over to meet him before his birthday this month." He shot her his best steely look as a way to belie everything mushy he felt inside. Dammit all, but he refused to let her see through this.

"Yeah, that was gonna be you, babe," he said. "Only one date and one Mother's Day weekend get-together to go. But I guess I'll need to pick up someone else now. No need to hold your breath or anything. You're off the hook."

Tears filled her eyes, but he didn't see them fall. Maybe she couldn't allow that. Maybe pride was working on her too.

"I see," she whispered. "I hope your cousin will still give you t-the money, I guess, if that's what you'd been planning on. The clinic is such a good cause. I, um, well, if you need someone to take to meet him—to prove, um, whatever, I could go—"

"Oh, no, sweetheart. Bingley is a bright guy. He'd see through a scam like that in a second. He'd know right away we weren't really a couple." He turned fast on his heel and strode to the door. He wanted to wipe every shred of pity off her beautiful little face. Glancing back at her one last time, he saw that he had. She looked sad, despondent even, but not the least bit sorry for him. It was a hollow victory, but a victory nonetheless.

"Goodbye," he said before closing the door behind him. He didn't give her a chance to answer.

***

Beth stared at the door. It still vibrated from Will's slamming of it. Not that he hadn't had a reason to be angry. In fact, under the circumstances, he'd behaved himself rather well. Except for the bet he'd flung in her face.

Oh, that hurt…but only because it had the ring of truth to it. She remembered with 20/20 hindsight all the information he'd told her about the clinic. The money they still needed. The ideas he'd had for it. The way he'd tried to gauge her interest and potential involvement. The passion that had shown on his face when he spoke of his project. It was as though Will was in the midst of a love affair, all right, but it was between him and his clinic, not between the two of them.

This explained his curiosity about her in a way that even her fictitious Love Match profile did not. Of course he'd need some pressing reason to pretend to be attracted to someone like her. Will Darcy would never have sought her out after that first coffee date without an ulterior motive, even if she'd actually *been* Charlotte Lucas. After all, most details about herself she hadn't been able to change.

She still had her average, twenty-six-year-old face.

She still dressed too humbly for someone with his sense of sophistication and style.

She still spoke with the same soft voice, which probably bored him without her realizing it.

"Charlotte" might have had more polish in her career and her lifestyle, but there'd been too much Beth Bennet in her from the beginning. It was all so clear now how foolishly she'd behaved. Will must have seen her as tiresome from the start, even before he found out about her real life.

The tears she'd held back while he was in her apartment began to fall in splashes on her shirt. She brushed some away with her sleeve, but soon that got too soaked to do much good. She grabbed a wad of tissues along with the research paper she'd written for her sociology class. It was due tomorrow afternoon.

She read over the monstrosity. The thing was dull and evasive by turns. She knew she could do better on it. After her talk with Will today, only about half the paper still felt legitimate anyway. She marked up the first five pages with corrections and more emotionally valid observations. Then she ripped the last five pages to shreds, the way she'd wanted to do this morning, and began rewriting.

Regardless of the grade Professor O'Reilly would give her, this time she was going to tell the truth, the whole truth and nothing but the truth. No matter what the consequences.

***

Will's insides were still shaking an hour later at the Koffee Haus. Granted, a double Dark Espresso Roast could make anyone jittery, but he knew better than to blame the beverage.

Beth Bennet—*that* was who to blame. For getting him to care about her. For making him feel like a fool. For pitying him, even for a few seconds, because she'd hoodwinked him. It was the first time since he was ten that he'd gotten sideswiped like this. Not since the year he'd overheard the school social worker whispering to a teacher about his "unfortunate home life." Will shook his head and swallowed the dregs of his coffee in one bitter gulp. Punishment he deserved.

He ordered another to go and drove back to Regents. He was off duty until tomorrow, but his choices for free time were limited to his cold condo, his mother's House of Tea and Inquiry, wandering around the city of Chicago with a chip on his shoulder or going to the hospital to work on raising funds for the clinic.

So, really, there was only one choice.

He guzzled half his drink on the walkway to the Regents business wing when he spotted Lang again by that same blasted tree. No one else was in sight, but this time the med student was openly sobbing. Cripes.

"Lang, what happened, man?"

Lang sniffled and turned away from him. "I apologize, Dr. Darcy. I thought I was alone."

"It's okay, I won't tell anyone. What's going on? Is it your third-floor patient again?"

He nodded, but Will only saw the back of his dark head. "She died a half hour ago. I—I just needed some time to get used to the idea." He turned back toward Will, his eyes glistening with raw pain. "I know you think I'm being overemotional about this, that I'll need to get tougher if I'm going to be a good doctor. I want to have thicker skin, I really do, but this lady was special. She really got to know me. While I was inside helping the others clean her up and take out the tubes, I had to pretend to be objective and indifferent. Strong, you know?"

Will nodded. He knew.

"But," Lang said, "she wasn't just a body to analyze. She touched me. She was the first patient that made me feel like I'd done some good. Like I wasn't just another medical student practicing on her. She saw *me*, even with all my inexperience. And I saw *her*, even with her lousy arteries and her blotchy skin and her heart condition. We were real people connecting, and it's not like that with everyone. I—I'm going to miss her."

Will put a hand on Lang's forearm. "I know you are. I'll bet you were one of the most pleasant parts of her last days, too. She might've hung around a little longer just because of you. Because you cared so much," he said, realizing it was probably true. Realizing how long it'd been since he'd let himself feel that way about a patient himself.

Lang broke into fresh sobs and buried his head in his hands. Will mutely patted his arm.

"I'll be okay, Doc," the med student muttered. "Please, just give me a few minutes alone."

With a final squeeze, Will let go. "Okay, Lang. Hang in there, though. You're heart is in the right place. That's gotta count for something."

"Thank you," the young man whispered.

Will's emotions danced around inside of him in a way that had been foreign for years. Yeah, he'd had too much coffee. Yeah, he hadn't gotten enough sleep in days. Yeah, every single person around him was getting all teary-eyed over something. If he didn't know himself better, he'd think he was turning into one of those emotional geysers himself. A disturbing part of his soul wanted to.

At this thought, an unfamiliar pain gripped his chest, begging for release. But it was like frostbite around his heart—the ache only turned torturous when it began to thaw. While he was numb, everything was cool. There were no problems. As long as he stayed detached, he couldn't feel the sting.

He lobbed his empty coffee cup in the trash and burst through the business office doors. Enough of this nonsensical thinking. He had a clinic to save and, somehow or other, he was going to figure out a way to do that. With or without Bingley's help.

**

Beth told Mrs. Moratti about her extra days off this week when she picked up Charlie at the usual time.

"S'everything okay, Beth?" She gave her a worried look. "You alright, then?"

"Oh, yes." Beth embraced the older lady. "I'll be fine, but I'll have a lot of work to do still during these next couple days. Could we keep Charlie's schedule with you the same as it's been?"

"Of-a course." Mrs. Moratti squeezed Charlie tight in emphasis.

"Hey, ow!" her little boy said, wrangling free. "You're gonna squash me like a pancake."

She and Mrs. Moratti laughed at his incensed

expression before Beth ruffled Charlie's hair and they left. She noticed a scrape on his elbow. "What's this from?" she asked.

"Recess. Mikey and I thought we'd play pirates, but the tree was gigantic, and I fell."

"The tree? Sweetheart, what kind of pirate spends his time in a tree?"

He looked at her like she was a dense as a mud ball. "Mom, I was Blackbird. Everyone's heard of Blackbird the Pirate."

She laughed. She couldn't help it. "I think you mean Black*beard*, honey." She planted a kiss on the top of his beloved little head.

"Well, that's who I was," he said, sounding indignant. "And I was real tough. A real man."

Beth swallowed. "Real men don't always have to be real tough to be brave. I know how amazing you are even when you're not being tough."

He turned those gorgeous eyes on her, so big, so open, so without fear. "Really, Mommy?"

"Yes, my darling. Really."

***

Smoke wafted out from underneath Professor O'Reilly's office door. Beth stood in the hallway, trying to decide whether she had the courage to knock or whether she should just slip the paper in the crack between the door and the floor tiles and then run. Finally, she lifted her fist and wrapped on the hard wood.

"C'mon in, who's ever out there," a gruff voice called.

She poked her head inside. "Hello, Professor," she said. "Sorry to disturb you, but I wanted to turn in my paper in person."

He raised both bushy white eyebrows and took a puff on his pipe. "Hope you don't mind the smoke, Miss

Bennet," he said, and it was clear to Beth that whether or not she objected to pipe smoke, she was going to get a lungful if she hung around.

The curtains billowed from the Professor's exhalations, and the throw rug all but coughed when Beth walked on it.

"That's all right, sir. I won't be staying for long." She handed him the large brown envelope with her final Sociology 369 paper inside. "I—I did the best I could on this, but I'm afraid I didn't end up proving what I'd set out to."

He laughed long and hardy. "Ah, Miss Bennet, your hypothesis was null and void, was it?"

She nodded. "I thought I'd found a case study that was as clear-cut as possible for my research. I did what was expected of me. I stated my objective, sought out a reasonable circumstance where it could be proven true and began observations. But—"

"But your initial hypothesis was wrong and, thus, you didn't get the anticipated results in return," he said. It was a statement, not a question.

She looked down at her worn shoes, feeling all the misery weighing on her more than ever. "Yes. I'm sorry."

He laughed again. "Don't be sorry. Hypotheses were meant to be proven true *or* false. Sometimes in academia the snobbiest of the snobs forget that. They get all worked up about their papers, about having something to publish, that they don't try anything daring. They stop reaching. And when a sociologist stops reaching, the results might be more predictable, but they're rarely very revealing or inspiring." He gave her a searching glance. "Looks like you actually learned something from your research, Miss Bennet, didn't you?"

Boy, did she ever. "Yes, sir. I really did."

"Well, good. That's the 'science' part. Now the big question—did you learn anything that you could actually apply to your life and your relationships?"

She considered his question and nodded. "More than you could possibly imagine."

"Excellent." He puffed on his pipe. "That's the 'social' part. And what do these two parts add up to, young lady?"

Beth couldn't help but feel warmth at his compassionate line of reasoning. "Social science, Professor," she answered dutifully.

"Ah-ha. So, from my vantage point there's not a thing to be sorry about. And, since you're a future social worker, I reckon an experience like this could only help you gain a better perspective on your field. It's always a good thing when we're forced to question our prejudices and stereotypes. To hold them under scrutiny and see if they measure up when they're put to the test. And if they don't, well…" He waited for her, indicating with a nod of his head that she should add her own thoughts.

"And if they don't," she began, "then we know we need to reevaluate. To see a person or circumstance more clearly. More objectively. Or, if we can't, to at least acknowledge how subjective our view is. How limited our perspective. How emotional and not particularly logical we all can be." Some of the sadness in her heart lifted when she said those words aloud. She smiled at Professor O'Reilly. "Especially when we have to face what we most fear about ourselves."

He waved the brown envelope in the air. "I suspect the paper inside here will be an A. But I sincerely hope, Miss Bennet, that you put more stock in, as you say, 'seeing more clearly' than you will in an honor-roll placement or even your degree. Life lasts long after school ends." He gave her a warm grin then all but shoved her out the door. "You made me forget my pipe for five whole minutes. Go on with you. Let me puff in peace."

"Thank you, Professor." She walked out into the shockingly fresh air of the hallway.

He raised a hand and said, "Best of luck, my dear," before shutting the door. A new batch of smoke began drifting out through the crack. She exhaled slowly in relief and headed to her car.

To celebrate this last academic milestone before graduation, she decided to treat herself to a specialty coffee at the Koffee Haus. Of course, she wasn't fooling herself. She hoped she might run into Will Darcy there. Kind of.

She also kind of hoped she wouldn't.

Her feelings were inconsistent. One minute she wished that Will would find love and happiness without her because she knew she'd hurt him and he deserved to be with someone who hadn't. Two minutes later, she wished he'd admit to an overwhelming love for her and would forgive her because only true love would make that possible. Most of the other minutes she just wished the ache in her heart would stop.

When she entered the coffee shop she scanned it, from window to window, tile to tile, to make sure she'd see Will if he were lurking in a back corner. He wasn't anywhere in sight. Darn it. But the aroma inside was enticing, nonetheless, and being here brought back memories as bittersweet as the chocolate in the cookies Will had gotten for them on that very first date.

Beth felt an almost genuine smile tug at the edges of her lips. It wasn't much, but it was a start. She stepped up to the counter to order.

"Do I know you?" a male voice asked from behind her.

Beth swiveled to look back at the guy. Tall, early thirties, dark hair, chiseled face. If it weren't for the greenish eyes and the somewhat egotistical look that marked him as someone other than Will, the two would've been convincing as brothers.

"I don't think so," she said, feeling a wariness creep into her pores. The guy *did* look familiar, though, even without his resemblance to Will. Her apprehensive nerve fibers began to skitter around.

He shook his head. "This isn't a line. I know I've seen you. You hang out here much?"

"I'm not a regular."

"Hmm. Too bad," she heard him mutter.

"What'll you have, ma'am?" the girl behind the counter asked.

"I, um, well…" She'd planned to get a small decaf, but being here made her want to be more adventurous, to try one of the flavors Will was so wild about.

"The Kona's to die for," the guy behind her whispered.

She nodded and ordered that, remembering how Will had mentioned it in his last email to her. The email before he found out she wasn't really Charlotte Lucas. She sighed and thanked the guy, still trying to place him.

"No problem. I practically live at this place. I read the paper here in the morning…or in the afternoon if I don't get to it soon enough." He let loose a short laugh, then ordered a Kona coffee of his own.

A few dozen light bulbs went off in her brain. That very first date with Will there'd been a guy who looked like him, reading the newspaper. The guy who disappeared right before Will entered. It must've been this man.

"You know, I think I remember you now," she said to him while they waited for their coffees. "I was here one afternoon last month to meet someone. It was kind of a blind date, so I spent a lot of time looking around the room, trying to find a person who matched the guy's description. Your features were, um, close to his. So, I must have been staring at you that day. I apologize."

"Ah, well, that wouldn't have been a problem from my standpoint," he said with a wink.

The coffees came and the Will-Look-Alike Guy confidently pointed his cup in the direction of a table, seeming sure she'd join him.

Well, he was right. She did. Not because she thought she'd start dating someone new, but because she felt an odd connection to him. It was as though he brought a piece of Will back to her.

He took a swig of his hot drink and looked her over carefully. Beth felt assessed, as though every element of her appearance was being itemized and catalogued. But she also realized there was something else behind this guy's almost arrogant exterior. She sensed a longing in his eyes. And when she softened toward him that little bit, she smiled. His expression changed. His eyebrows shot up, and he choked on some coffee.

"Oh, good Lord. Will's gonna kill me," he whispered.

Now *her* eyebrows shot up, and the coffee in her mouth went down too fast, like liquid fire, making her cough and sputter.

"Will?" she managed to say. "You...you know him?"

CHAPTER TEN

"I didn't recognize you until you smiled," the guy said, shaking his head and clawing a bit at his throat. "Oh, man. Will would skin me alive for almost flirting with you." He reached over and put a couple of gentle fingers on Beth's wrist. "Please don't tell him. I'd be in deep trouble with my workaholic cousin."

Her heart leaped in her chest higher than a bird in the sky. It raced faster than a jet plane. Then it stopped, weighted down by kryptonite and the certainty that Superman wouldn't be coming to her rescue on this one. "Y-you're Bingley?"

"You bet'cha, gorgeous." He glanced around. "So, where's Cuz? Hospital's only a few blocks away. Is he coming here to meet you?"

Didn't Will tell him about their breakup? She took a deep breath. If Will had a chance of still winning his bet, she'd better not let on to his cousin about what'd happened until she knew what Bingley knew. "No, not this time," she said cautiously. "When did you last speak with him?"

Bingley shrugged. "Few days back. He showed me a nice photo of you two at his mom's place." He grinned. "What'd you think of Aunt Angie? She's a piece of work, eh?"

Heavens. It was true. Bingley wasn't aware her relationship with Will had ended. Well, maybe in her small way, she could help Will out. Try to make up for lying to him by figuring out a way to secure the funding for his clinic. She pasted on her most winning smile.

"Angie was great," she said in an overenthusiastic voice. "As warm and welcoming as if I were a member of the family."

Bingley's teeth flashed and his eyes sparkled. "If my aunt has her way, you will be. The woman's afraid to say it aloud, but she's itching to be a grandmother."

She raised a brow. "And so she's encouraging Will to look for a wife of childbearing age and inclination?"

"Hell, no. That dude's such a workaholic, it's a virtual miracle he even went out on a date. You're the first woman he's been serious about since—I can't even remember how long." Bingley gave her another of his scrutinizing glances. "He's so, so…careful with his heart. Keeps too much of himself closed up so the world can't splatter him with its dust and grime."

"How do you mean?"

"It's like he squirted himself all over with butter-flavored cooking spray. He comes across as genuine and enticing, but nobody can stick to him. Part of it is his medical persona. He needs to keep a certain distance from tragedy and illness to be effective. Or so he says. A lot of it is just Will and his self-protection system."

"Because of not having a father around?" she said, thinking about Charlie and whatever unexpressed feelings of loss he must have because of Pete's absence.

Bingley shrugged. "Yeah, that. But mostly because of the kinds of guys Aunt Angie hooked up with years ago. Will's two stepfathers were real nutcases. Cruel to him in subtle ways. He was just a kid then and couldn't see them for the jerks they were. He allowed himself to get attached, but their acceptance of him was always conditional. They interacted with him only when his mother insisted upon it and, even then, not very warmly."

"Hmm, yes. He told me that." As always, whenever Beth thought about it, her heart went out to the little boy Will once was. "But Will never struck me as someone cold or aloof. Is that how you see him?"

"Not at all. Not with the people he loves and trusts, but that's a pretty tiny circle. He always acts responsibly toward everyone, but he doesn't allow himself to get emotionally involved anymore. People rarely get under his skin because he doesn't give them the opportunity to penetrate. He's got a defense shield NATO couldn't breech."

And yet, Beth realized, she'd breeched it. If he hadn't been affected by her, he wouldn't have stormed her apartment. He wouldn't have been so angry. She felt her first sliver of hope.

"He's so driven by his work to get the clinic up and running, though," she said. "Maybe, once he's gotten it established, he'll feel content with his accomplishments. Maybe he'll naturally drop his guard then."

Bingley snorted. "Not likely. I keep forgetting you don't know him as well as I do. At least not yet. You two have been on, what? Four dates, right?"

"Right," she admitted, then instantly regretted it. She remembered Will saying he needed to get to five dates, plus a one-on-one meeting with Bingley, before winning the bet. Maybe she should've said five or even six dates.

She opened her mouth to contradict herself, but thought better of it. She'd lied enough and, besides, Will wouldn't be able to pretend an affection for her now.

Bingley didn't seem to notice her hesitation.

"My cousin's been on a mission to right the injustices heaped on him and his mom back in the days when money was scarce and compassion for single mothers even scarcer," he said. "The guy can't go back in time and fix all the wrongs. The medical services they couldn't afford. The fine dining or tasty extras like gourmet coffee they couldn't splurge on. So, instead, he wages his wars in every moment of every day."

Bingley slurped the last of his coffee and lobbed the cup into the nearby trash bin. "This clinic, however awesome, won't allay Will's demons. Not 'til he gets a ton of perspective on his past and at least an ounce of balance in his present."

"And you hoped to help him get it, didn't you?" she said, suddenly understanding.

He lifted his lips in a very convincing smirk. "Yep."

"What did you do?"

He shook his head. "You'll hate me if I tell you. And Will would turn his fury on me so fast I'd be lucky to keep my head intact. I'd never feel safe being alone with him again, what with the way he can wield a scalpel and all." He twisted a napkin on the table. "Nope. I'll just have to leave you guessing."

Talking with Will's cousin wasn't remotely the experience she'd expected, not that she'd anticipated ever running into the wealthy and mysterious Bingley. But with this opportunity came a newfound responsibility.

She tossed caution to the wind and met his eye. "Bingley, as of this week, Will and I are no longer together. I wish we were, but we're not." Without using names, she briefly told him what had transpired between her and his cousin. "What I need to know is this—what can I do to help Will get the money you promised him for the clinic?"

She saw his face turn pale and his mouth drop open. She held up her hand to stop his comments. "I know I'm not supposed to know about your bet, but I do. Will fully believes the clinic's funding is riding on five dates with a woman plus attendance at some pre-birthday get-together of yours. I'm guessing it's more than that. What are you really after?"

He buried his head in his hands. "Oh, man, I can't believe he told you about the matchmaking bet." He looked her in the eye. "I'm surprised, and I'm also sorry if you feel caught in the middle of this. It's not entirely what you think."

What the heck could she think? She raised her palms at him. "So, enlighten me."

He leaned over the table toward her then slunk back against his chair again. "Can't do it. I'll tell you this much, though—Aunt Angie and I have been trying to get Will to open up for years. All above board. Not a single bribe or underhanded scheme involved. But nothing worked. This time, though, we thought we had a sure shot. He wanted the clinic. We wanted him to date. He needed the money. We had it. Easy as pie."

"We? You mean you and Angie were in on this together?"

"In a manner of speaking, yes. Aunt Angie is my mom's younger sister. Mom didn't have much money when she married my dad, but after a decade or so he started to do well in banking. Then he got into investing and things really took off. I got a trust fund out of it when I was eighteen, and I learned a lot about making money from the comfort of my La-Z-Boy." He played with a red stirring stick, tapping it against the table.

"My aunt and Will got by okay financially," he said. "But she'd never hear of accepting any cash gifts from my family. Before Mom and Dad moved to Tuscany, Mom told me to keep an eye out for her sister and for Will. And not just in a financial sense."

"Wait, your folks live in *Italy?*" Jeez, and she thought her parents were far away because they'd moved to Phoenix.

"Yeah. Nice place to visit. Great climate. And they come back for holidays and important social occasions like weddings...or Macy's super sales." He grinned at her. "I'm telling you, my parents are really rich."

She only nodded. These were people who ate spaghetti by choice, not because it was cheap. Must make all the difference in the world having it served by a five-star chef in a Florentine villa.

She glanced at Bingley more closely. The immaculate grooming, the high-quality clothing, the air of privilege—maybe this was what contributed to his appearance of arrogance. When she was talking to him, though, he seemed much less snobbish. More compassionate somehow.

"We know how to grow money," he said, "which was my point. Aunt Angie and I had a chat. We wanted him to open up, date a bit, try to give love a chance. Aunt Angie knows I can throw a lot of cash Will's way if he's willing to take a risk but, we agreed, *only* then." He shrugged. "If he's not, the dude's out of luck. I, for one, have got no patience for wimps."

"But this clinic would help so many people, Bingley, and—"

"My game, my rules. No argument."

She clenched her fingers until her nails bit into her palms. "So, I can't convince you? Nothing I say has any weight in 'your game'?" She felt the flush of anger rise on her cheeks and immediately took back her thoughts about his compassionate nature. Only, there were vibes from him she couldn't account for. She wasn't able to figure whose side he was on.

"'Fraid not, darling. My interest is in studying Will. In his behavior. His actions and reactions. He's the one who needs to do the convincing. I'll keep your comments in mind, though." He squinted at her. "You still like my cousin then, huh?"

"Yes," she whispered, realizing now that there was no way Will would ever need her, not even to win a stupid bet. She couldn't help him even by doing him the smallest of favors.

Bingley confirmed this. "What happens next is Will's show, sunshine. The money I promised him for the clinic is his *only* if he lives up to his end of the bargain. Unless he lets down his guard and gets serious about someone, all bets are off. No pun intended." He chuckled. "Man, and I even offered to double the stakes if he proposed to you—"

"*YOU WHAT?*"

He raised a brow at her and sighed. "Yeah, well, so much for that strategy. I thought, once he plunged into the dating world again, he might find a reason to stay. A reason that had nothing to do with his all-consuming clinic. Don't feel bad, sweet pea. You were the closest he ever came." He shrugged. "Win some, lose some, I guess."

She appraised the facial expression of the man before her. Despite his nonchalant appearance, Bingley seemed anything but indifferent to the outcome. It was clear he'd wanted her relationship with Will to succeed, even if he'd be out several million as a result. Odd fellow.

And, if she'd read him right, he seemed to crave a happily-ever-after Love Match for himself, too. She should probably introduce him to Jane... Heck, her best friend might actually *like* this loony bird.

Beth's romance with Will was a ridiculous fantasy, though, at least on her part. As if Will would have actually proposed to her! She hugged her arms to her chest.

He wouldn't have, would he?

No.

And, if he did, it would have been for the sake of the clinic, not for her. People just didn't get in life what they fantasized about, Perfect Match or no. And, in her case, she knew she'd never get that yearned-for man who would love her forever, just as she was. And who would love Charlie, too.

"Thank you for explaining, Bingley. I appreciate your candor." She gave him a weak smile. "I wish I'd been as irresistible to Will as you'd hoped. But I guess some of that is my own fault. I hope your upcoming birthday will be a happy one." She stood up and prepared to leave.

"Thanks. Nice meeting you," he said.

She dumped her trash in the bin then played with the sleeves of her blouse. "You, too," she said, surprised that, in spite of everything, this was true.

"Hey." He cleared his throat and gave her a sheepish grin. "I feel like a clod for bringing this up now but, um, what's your name? You probably don't want me calling you doll face or sugarplum or something like that anymore."

She grimaced.

"I thought not," he said. "Will never told me who you were, though. He just let me call you the Love-Match

Lady. And here I stupidly talked to you for over a half hour and didn't think to ask your real name."

Her real name. The irony of this question struck her hard. "Beth," she said on her way out to hunt down that stubborn cousin of his. "It's Beth Ann Bennet."

***

Beth saw the familiar tuft of dark hair that belonged to Will's head as she peered across the hospital cafeteria at him. His back was to her and he was conversing with another doctor. She forced herself to take four, then five, then six steps in his direction.

The other doctor strode away. Beth froze.

She watched Will stab at some mystery casserole on his plate, his gaze fixed on the smudged tabletop. She gulped as much oxygen as her lungs could hold and pushed on toward him.

"Will," she whispered to his shoulders.

He spun around in the chair so fast that the wind he created propelled her backward. Or maybe it was fear that did it.

Their eyes met. He clutched his fork—which held a chunk of chicken or something on it—like a motionless sword against her. The yellowish sauce from the meat dripped on the tile between them, but he didn't move. Beth was incapable of anything resembling speech.

"I—um—" she tried.

His eyes narrowed.

"Could we—"

His lips tightened.

"Hmm, well, are you—"

His fingers fisted until the knuckles turned an unhealthy shade of alabaster.

This is going well. She gave up on coherence and just watched him glare at her.

Finally, he rose slowly from the chair. His legs unfolded beneath him, displaying limbs of lean muscle. All that power supporting him, the lucky man. Her knees were so weak she felt she might topple over at any moment.

His mouth opened.

"Calling Dr. Emrick and Dr. Darcy to the ER," a disembodied voice over the loudspeaker requested.

Will closed his mouth, dropped his fork to the plate with an extra-heavy clink and stalked off.

And that, as they'd say in baseball, was one big strikeout.

***

A day later, Beth stood outside Social Services, a few minutes early for her meeting with Dan Noelen. It was a beautiful spring day. She'd taken Charlie on his first stroller ride on a day like today. He'd been six weeks old then, a little peanut of a baby, and his eyes fluttered shut every time the wind blew on his face. She smiled, remembering.

Now he was six *years* old. Growing up and wanting the truth about his life and his past. She'd done the best she could with the resources she had. She would never have given him up, and she'd worked like crazy to keep their lives together and on track. It'd been hard, but she had nothing to regret. She wouldn't start regretting now.

She took a deep breath of fresh May air and marched into the building.

Dan opened his office door and got right to the point. "So, let's chat, Beth. Where are you with this?"

Beth exhaled slowly. "On the phone a few days back, you asked some very good questions. This has been a time of self-discovery for me, I guess, even though I hadn't planned it that way. I need to tell you the truth."

He looked concerned and brushed the thick hair away from his brow. "You've reconsidered taking the position, then?"

"I've considered and reconsidered every aspect of my life, Dan." She paused. "I did as you'd asked me to, but the conclusion I came to was the same." She steadied herself in her chair and looked him in the eye. "I want the position—if you'll have me and if I'm approved for it—and I very much want to be a social worker."

"Would you still want to be a social worker even if you're not on my team here?"

She panicked at his words. Darn it. So maybe he didn't want her back after all. Maybe he thought she was unstable or unreliable after everything that had happened. But she thought through his question despite the hurt. Even if she weren't working here, this was the job she loved to do. The career where she felt she made the most difference and where she felt her work was most rewarding. "Yes," she said. "Even then."

He nodded. "Why?"

"Because it's who I am. It's the path that's right for me. True, it's a lot of work for a modest wage, but every day I'd be doing something I believed in. Something I'm sure will be of help to people because it was such a great help to me." She smiled at him then added, "But the greater truth is that I love being with the elderly. They're wise and bright and have wonderful stories to share. I have so much to learn from them, and there are so many lessons in life that need learning. Like being honest about yourself. Like taking risks with your heart. Like being proud of the challenges you've overcome."

Dan rubbed his hand on his chest in the vicinity of his heart. "They've got a lot to share, but so do you, Beth."

"Thank you."

"I'll be recommending you to the board at their June first meeting."

Her stomach flipped and her soul bounded up and did a jig. "You're keeping me on here after all?"

"Of course, kiddo. Didn't want to lose you if I didn't have to. Now," he pointed his finger at her, "is there anything you want to tell me about your Dr. Will Darcy? Any reason I shouldn't trust him or want to remain the social services consultant for his project?"

"No, Dan. He and I may have had a falling out, but his clinic is a great idea. I wish it'd been there for me when Charlie was born. Please, support him any way you can but, if you would, keep me off that case. I haven't yet learned enough life lessons to deal with the Good Doctor face to face anytime soon."

***

Will stuck his head under the stainless-steel hospital faucet and flipped on the tap. Ice-cold water gushed over his hair, matting it in a manner no one but his mother would consider attractive.

Nah, even Mom would think he looked awful.

He fluffed it dry with a paper towel and rubbed the sleep out of his eyes for the third consecutive day this week. He had to stop taking on these extra shifts, but it was the only way to keep Beth's wounded eyes from haunting him.

"Hey, hey. What's up, Cuz?"

Bingley's too cheerful voice at the door was an unhappy reminder that Will's clinic project was in shambles. Maybe, between his own large donation and some new avenues of funding, he'd be able to raise the minimum capital by Christmas instead of by his original spring deadline. He looked at his calendar. Not that he didn't know the date. Today was Mother's Day.

"Don't you know how to knock?" Will glared at his cousin.

Bingley shrugged. "What's the fun in that?"

"Oh, I don't know. Maybe respect could be *fun* for a change. Or privacy. Or courtesy. Or any of the qualities you lack." He knew he was spoiling for a fight and, fair or unfair, there was no one on the planet he wanted to punch out more than Bingley at the moment.

His cousin leveled one of his rare worried looks his way. "Um, well, maybe this is a bad time."

"Damn right it's a bad time. What d'ya want, Bingley? Come in here to gloat?"

"No. Just checking in. See how you're doing." He squinted those green eyes at him. "You okay, Will?"

Bingley almost never called him Will. He must look like he was on death's door for his golf-playing, bet-making, ultra-casual cousin to resort to formalities.

"I'm fine," he said, opening a drawer, pulling out a comb and slamming the drawer shut. "And a happy freaking birthday to you."

Bingley flinched. "Alrighty. I'm going." He took two steps back and grabbed the doorknob.

Will sighed. "Wait. Bingley, stop. Please."

His cousin paused. "Sorry I bothered you."

"Nah, forget it. I apologize. I'm just in a really crummy mood." *And it wouldn't take a genius to guess why.* Will held out his hand to Bingley. "Are we okay, man? Can I buy you a meal or something for your birthday?" He glanced at his watch, which still looked blurry through his sleep-deprived eyes. "I mean later. Sometime after noon?"

Bingley grasped his palm none too gently. "We're okay, and I'll take a rain check on the food." His cousin's gaze darted around the room then returned to Will's face. "Have you seen your Love-Match Lady lately? Got any more cute Polaroid snapshots?"

Will's blood started pumping as if he'd had to single-handedly deal with a multiple-car-crash trauma instead of merely a few questions about an ex-girlfriend. "No, on both counts," he said, hoping Bingley would knock it off. Couldn't he read the signs? Know just from looking at him that things with his "Love Match" were over?

"Well, when am I going to meet her?" his cousin asked, clearly lacking even garden-variety intuition.

"Never."

Bingley stared blankly at him, mocking him just by the way he stood. So curious. So carefree. "What do you mean—*never?* You were so serious about her. I thought she might've been The One for you. And today's the final day, you know."

"I know," he muttered. He turned away before his cousin could grow some empathy and read the pain that surely radiated off his face. "I thought she might've been The One, too, but we broke up."

"Why?"

Now here was a question that, despite the obvious facts, Will still couldn't answer to his satisfaction. "She wasn't who she said she was," he said. How else could he explain?

"Were you who you said you were?" Bingley asked him.

"What?"

"Were *you,* when you started all this Love Match stuff, the person you presented yourself to be?"

"Well, I didn't lie about my identity," Will said. But, upon a little reflection, he amended this. "So, okay, I didn't exactly put my reasons for dating on the table right away. I was, I suppose, kind of dishonest, too, but—"

Bingley had the audacity to laugh. "You can't be 'kind of' dishonest, Cuz. You're either telling the truth or you're lying. No real in between there."

Now where had he heard those oh-so-wise words before? He ran the comb through his hair in seven vicious strokes, grimacing when he hit the tangles. "It would never have worked anyway," he said.

"Why's that?"

"Why are you so damn curious?"

Bingley lifted his shoulders then let them drop. "Because I *care*, Cuz. Even if you don't think so."

Will gave him a long, hard stare. Bingley seemed sincere, but this didn't completely override Will's suspicion of his cousin or his depression at losing the woman he'd come to love. He studied the floor tiles and sighed.

"Why wouldn't it have worked?" Bingley asked again.

"Because we started on the wrong foot. We both had secrets we didn't share. We both played games with the other's time and emotions. And we didn't stay in the ring long enough to battle it all out." He threw his hands up in the air before clenching them into fists. "It can't be fixed, so I lose your bet, and you don't owe me a red cent. Happy now?"

Bingley shook his head. "Wouldn't say so, Cuz."

Will wanted to bury his head in his palms and weep like a two year old but, of course, he didn't. Grown men couldn't back down and cry. Not even when they were hurt. He gritted his teeth. "What would you say?"

"I'd say I'm confused on something. I've got a question."

"Well, what?"

"You look like you did the day your first patient died.

Like you'd really lost something precious to you that couldn't be replaced or retrieved." Bingley shed his jester-like enthusiasm for a whole minute and looked him in the eye, dead serious. "Which was the biggest loss—the money for the clinic or the love of the girl?"

"They're both losses, Bingley."

"No. I need a rank order on this one."

Will hung his head, his heart having answered the question in an instant, but his fool brain still struggling to come up with the right way to explain it.

"I love my clinic project," he began. "It's an idea I conceived, and I'm this close to bringing it to completion." He brought his index finger and thumb to within a millimeter of each other. "It'd be a dream come true to have a place where low-income moms could go to find affordable healthcare for themselves and their kids. I'd finally feel I'd done something important in my life. You understand that, Bingley, right?"

"Right."

Will traced his eyebrows with his fingertips. "But...the woman I met brought a new dream to me. I— I didn't expect that. Any of it. But she just *got to me*, you know?"

"I know," Bingley said.

"And now I can't get rid of these feelings. She unfroze me or something, but the damage is done. I can't refreeze what she'd thawed."

His cousin grinned. "So, let me get this straight. Though the clinic's critically important to you, a part of you just can't help but be devastated by the loss of this woman—"

"I wouldn't say 'devastated.' I mean I don't look that bad, do I?"

Bingley raised a dubious eyebrow.

Oh, great. That was all he needed. His cousin thinking he was a basket case over some cute chick. Okay, beautiful, warm-hearted woman. With, he shouldn't forget, a truckload of lies alongside her and a six-year-old kid hanging out at home. And, hell, even if he was turning into a basket case, why couldn't he put her out of his mind for five lousy minutes?

"So," Bingley said, "between the money or Beth, you'd have chosen Beth—because you love her?"

Will nodded. It was senseless to deny it, and his cousin looked smugly satisfied by the news. But something odd tugged at Will's unfocused mind. He tapped his forehead a few times before realization came flooding in.

"Hey," he said to Bingley, "how'd you know her name was Beth?"

CHAPTER ELEVEN

"Happy Mother's Day, Mom." Will stomped into his mother's feng-shui-perfect house a few hours later and held out a huge bouquet of wildflowers. Less cliché than roses, he decided. "I figured I'd better come over now if I wanted to see you. Bingley told me you were headed out for the evening."

"I am?" She admired the flowers, put them in a crystal vase.

"Aren't you?"

"Aren't I what?" She returned to her chair to fiddle with the stitches on her latest embroidery. A vegetable cornucopia, it looked like. She tugged on the green thread for one of the tiny peppers. It snapped, and the split end hung limply from her needle. "Darn it all," she mumbled.

"Aren't you going out tonight?" He strode over to her, covering her shaking hand with his. "What's going on, Mom? Did Bingley get his facts wrong again?"

She smiled wanly at him. "Bingley. Who knows what that boy was thinking? He probably just wanted to slip away from you and thought I'd make a good distraction.

And, no, I'm not going anywhere unless you're planning to take me out to dinner or, better yet, to lunch in a half hour."

"It's a date," he said. Then, squeezing her fingers a little tighter, he whispered, "Please let me know what I can do for you. You've got me worried."

She kissed his cheek. "Have some tea with me."

He nodded and strolled outside onto the "English garden." He tossed his exhausted body in one of the sturdy, floral-cushioned patio chairs and closed his eyes.

He'd been on the verge of doing it all. Of accomplishing the once impossible task of beating the system and getting medical aid to those who needed it most. No young mother, no little child, would have been left wanting on his watch, that was for sure.

He opened his eyes again, glared at a few chipmunks who dared to scamper too close to his feet and studied his mom through the screen door as she busied herself with tea-making in the kitchen. She seemed out of sorts today. Then again, so was he.

"Herbal Red Raspberry?" she called out.

"Sure, thanks." He thought of Bingley's admission of meeting Beth and wished for a triple shot of espresso along with the tea.

Mom brought it out to him a few minutes later— caffeine-free, unfortunately. "So, I haven't heard you talk about your lovely lady friend, Charlotte. How's she doing?" His mother's blue eyes had turned so bright and hopeful on him, his heart sank like a boulder all over again.

He took a deep breath and a sip of weak tea. "Well, Mom," he said. "First of all, her name's Beth—not Charlotte. She didn't tell me her real name until…recently."

His mom looked taken aback for a second, then she became very still. "Did she have a reason for withholding that information?"

Will thought about it. "In a manner of speaking, I suppose she did. She also withheld the little tidbit about having a six-year-old son."

Her sharp blue eyes scanned his face. "Oh."

"That's all you're gonna say? *Oh?* C'mon, Mom. Time for some parental words of wisdom here."

His mother shrugged. "What's there to say? I know how you feel about us."

"What do you mean?"

"Us. Single mothers. We frighten you. You've got issues with us and with the whole complex relationship. You want your interactions with women to be direct. Streamlined. Clear-cut. Other men's children throw all that off kilter. Everything becomes scattered and confusing. It's hard work."

"Oh. That's what you mean."

She stood up and hugged him. "My baby boy. Just look at you now. So grown up and yet—"

"And yet what?"

"And yet you're still trying to fix my life, not your own. You're still trying to correct the past by manipulating the present. You might be able to get away with doing that in some areas. But not in any long-term relationships."

So, what was his mom trying to say? That he was responsible for wrecking his short-lived romance? That he was making of fool of himself? No newsflash there.

He explained Beth's background. The fact that she was going to be a social worker instead of a child psychologist. He told his mom about the research she was doing for her class and the humiliating way he discovered the truth. "Now that you know the whole story, give me some honest, well-informed advice."

A half smile played on her lips. She picked up her china cup and traced the patterns on the side. "Charlotte. Beth. Whatever her name is...I liked her. A lot. And she liked me, I could tell. She's not one of those condescending gals, so sure she's got all the answers just because her skin's still smooth and nothing on her body is drooping yet. She has respect for older people. You can just feel it. Someone like that can't be all bad."

"I didn't say I thought she was bad, I meant—"

"And she liked you, too," Mom insisted. "A mother can tell these things." She grinned openly. "And you, dear heart, liked her. Quite a bit, if I'm not mistaken."

He didn't bother with denials. He didn't have any. He just sighed loudly and hoped his mom would interpret it as exasperation not evasion.

But Mom was too good at this game. She touched his cheek with her fingertip, gentle compassion evident in her caress. "Oh, honey," she whispered. "If the good things, the big ones, are there between you, don't waste your time hashing over insignificant differences. Keep your focus on what matters most. Forget the rest and enjoy being with one another."

She closed her eyes, and Will could see the signs of aging taking place on her cheeks and chin. Neither of them were getting any younger, but he could feel how drained she was today. He hoped if his mother ever required a social worker's help in her life again, that person would be someone genuinely empathetic. Someone like Beth, he realized with a start.

But what kind of person did *he* need? Was it the type of woman he'd always thought he was looking for? Or was it Beth?

***

Beth wrestled with her luncheon taco, trying to keep the beef and the diced tomatoes from plopping out of its shell. Jane sat cross-legged on the carpet next to her, struggling with a similar problem, a piece of shredded lettuce clinging to her chin.

Jane licked her lips and swiped at her face with a napkin. "So, Dan seems to think you'll be a shoo-in when it comes to getting the board's approval, right?"

"He said he's never yet been turned down when the person up for review was someone he'd personally recommended." Beth's heart pounded and her hands shook with excitement just remembering her boss's words. "He said if there weren't any problems with my grades or my graduation, that I could pretty much count on having a full-time job in June."

Jane gave her a sideways hug. "That's awesome news."

She nodded. "Charlie will be in school all day once September hits, so I'll be able to work almost eight-hour days without the need for childcare. And no tuition payments. In another year or so, I should have enough saved up to move to a bigger apartment or maybe even buy a new car. Well, a new *used* car, but still..."

"You're on your way, baby."

"I hope so. Gosh, Jane, it's been such a long road. I can hardly believe—" She paused and took another bite of taco. It was too difficult to explain.

"You can hardly believe what?"

"That I made it through this on my own."

"Yeah," Jane said.

Beth caught a flicker of something she couldn't immediately identify in her friend's eye. Was it...hurt? And she thought about all the meals—like this one—that

Jane had brought over in the past few years. About all the times Jane babysat for Charlie while she ran an important errand. Or even a not-so-important errand. About all the help and encouragement Jane gave her when the struggles of being a single mom were overwhelming. Big things, little things. Jane was there for them all.

"You know," Beth said, "that's not exactly true, is it?"

"What's not true?"

"That I made it through on my own." She nodded in the direction of Charlie, who was slurping an orange soda across the room and adding a few finishing touches to the special Mother's Day drawing he'd made for her. "Bringing him up. I wasn't alone. You were as much a part of our family as if you'd really been Charlie's auntie."

A few tears glistened in Jane's eyes, but Beth saw her blink them away. "Aw, Beth—"

"Shhh. You know it's true." She threw an arm around Jane's shoulders and squeezed. "I owe a lot of people for their time and their help and their love. Mrs. Moratti's been amazing. Dan, Abby and Robby are always so supportive at work. But most of all you, Jane. You're the one who got me through the really tough times. You're the one who made me laugh. I'm so lucky you're my friend."

"We made it through together," Jane whispered. "After all, I don't have family around here anymore either, and I never had a sister." She sniffled and wiped the bottom of her nose with her crumpled napkin. "Always wanted one." Jane gave her a fierce hug then began humming the Sister Sledge tune "We Are Family," which made Beth giggle.

"You are such a goofball," Beth said.

"Yeah, yeah." Jane's eyes twinkled, but then she turned serious. "Look, you should be proud of what you've accomplished. Raising a son as great as that little monster." She pointed to Charlie and grinned. "Pete doesn't know what he missed out on."

"I know." But Beth wondered about Charlie, as she always did. Did he have an inkling of what he was missing out on by not having a dad? "Thanks for sharing this Mother's Day with me."

"You're very welcome. So, what's this week look like, schedule-wise?"

"Well," Beth said, "I've got my final visit at Mrs. Hammond's on Friday at two. Then I'll be officially done with my practicum."

"Super! We'll have to celebrate," Jane said. "Will Charlie be with Mrs. Moratti the whole afternoon?"

Beth wrinkled her nose. "He will if she gets back in time. She's got a dentist appointment late morning on Friday to have a crown put in. If she can't get out of there before I need to leave, I'll go in to Mrs. Hammond's over the weekend instead."

"Nah. Don't worry about it. I'm done with exams and don't have to start my summer job for a week. Why don't you tell Mrs. Moratti she's got Friday off? I can meet Charlie at the bus and take him to the park or the library or somewhere. Finish what you need to get done so we can have a celebratory weekend, okay?"

Beth grinned her thanks. "Okay."

***

Will had a lengthy confrontation planned with his cousin. As he drove away from his mom's house a few hours later, he began rehearsing dialogue in his Ferrari.

"Just for the record," Will said aloud to the imaginary Bingley, "explain something to me." He knew his tone would sound icy but, with his heart refreezing, it was to be expected. "What did you think would be accomplished by getting me to search the Love Match website?"

Bingley would stutter, mumble something incoherent about having Will's "best interests" in mind and slink off into the corner of the coffee shop or wherever they were meeting. Will would have to do everything in his power to keep from throwing the first punch at that secretive, arrogant, manipulative… He slammed his fist into the steering wheel, sending out a loud beep to the unsuspecting Ford Escort in front of him.

"Sorry," he mouthed to the driver as he passed her. The woman inside shot him a worried glance.

Will sighed. Could Bingley's behavior be anything but despicable? Maybe it could. The possibility of a benign motive was a tempting thing to hope for. After all, was it really *wrong* for his closest family members to want him to fall in love? To think he might be happier with a wonderful woman in his life, and not just his work obsessions?

Oh, brother.

He missed her. Beth. He couldn't keep denying it. It was Bingley's fault, though, for making him meet her. If Bingley hadn't come up with that harebrained bet, Will would have never actually gone online and created a Love Match profile.

He wouldn't have had to screen the hordes of women there, none of whom caught his attention like Charlotte Lucas, a.k.a. Beth Bennet.

He never would have gone out with her or watched the fading sunlight catch her hair.

He wouldn't have kissed her, held her hand in the darkened movie theater or introduced her to his mother.

He wouldn't have had to feel the extremes he was feeling. The elation. The agony. The desire. The despair. He could have stayed detached. Been emotionally untouchable.

And then he wouldn't be in the state he was in right now. Which was mad. Really mad.

Will shoved his car into park and bolted out of it. He hammered on Bingley's front door. The housekeeper answered.

"Yes, Dr. Darcy? How may I help you?" the middle-aged lady asked.

"I'd like to see my cousin. Now, if possible."

She gave him a pained look. "I'm sorry, sir. Mr. McNamara left town on business rather suddenly. He won't be back until Friday."

Left town? Armchair Money Man? Like hell he did, the coward. "I guess I'll see him Friday, then," Will told the woman stiffly. "Please tell him to contact me after he returns."

"Of course, sir."

Will left and impulsively drove to the public playground near Beth's apartment complex. He parked in the shadows and observed. Kids were climbing on the jungle gym and rolling around in the sandbox, their faces flushed with activity and innocence. Parents were scattered everywhere.

He scanned every inch of the fenced-in play area and, sure enough, there they were. Beth, who was talking to a redheaded woman, and the kid. Charlie.

Bingley's birthday would be over in a few hours, and the clinic's funding couldn't be saved now anyway. A part of him desperately wanted to call Beth over, to try to work something out between them, regardless of what had transpired before. But the odds seemed stacked against him.

Beth's life wouldn't revolve around the clinic like he'd once imagined.

Even if he succeeded in getting the money from some other source to fund it, which wouldn't be easy. Even if, somehow, he and Beth got together as a couple, which wouldn't be likely.

The two of them working side-by-side had been a nice fantasy while it lasted, but an unrealistic one. She'd constructed her world differently and, hey, maybe that wasn't such a bad thing all in all.

But then there was her son.

For all of Bingley's meddling, even he didn't try to lecture Will on this issue. Bingley didn't know what it was like to grow up with stepfathers. He didn't have firsthand experience with how crummy it could be to have to live with a doomed relationship like that.

Will knew it wouldn't be fair to take on such a role after what he'd gone through growing up. Not fair to himself, not to Beth and not to her little boy.

He watched Charlie swing on the monkey bars. He smiled as Beth and the other lady clapped for the kid while he performed gymnastic feats. He sat in the dark of his car and knew he shouldn't be there, like some sick voyeur casing a family he didn't belong to.

Will pulled out of the lot. He tried to hurry up the freeze on his heart but nothing, not even numbness, was cooperating today.

***

"How're ya, child?" Mrs. Hammond said to Beth Friday afternoon, her face a little red from the walk to the door. She ambled back to her easy chair once Beth was inside and began issuing instructions. "Git into the kitchen, girl. Pour you'self some lemonade."

"Thanks, Mrs. Hammond, I'd love some."

"Fresh squeezed, it is. I be complainin' to my grandson 'bout how I missed the tart taste of real lemon.

Told him his muscles needed buildin' up. How they could use a good flexin'. He got right on the job." She laughed. "Boys and men. They be all the same. Do anythin' if they think their manhood's in question."

Beth wanted to give her a big hug. In her unassuming way, Lynn Hammond knew more about human nature and gender-role stereotypes then all the PhDs in the Ivy League.

"How have you been feeling this week?" Beth said, pulling out her clipboard. "Are the services we set up last month working out for you? The Merry Maids?"

"Oh, them girls are great! Cleanin' up so fast, smilin' like they be enjoyin' themselves. Watchin' them's better than 'Wheel of Fortune.' Real entertainment, and I don't gotta do no more dusting. Always hated that."

Beth laughed. "Me, too. Well, I'm glad that's going well." She made a note of it on the page and asked about the meal delivery and a few other services provided.

When all of the required information was precisely recorded, Beth found herself relaxing as she usually did in Mrs. Hammond's company.

"I thought about you a lot in the past few weeks," she told the elderly lady. "Some of the things you said on our last visit really stuck with me."

"Don't you know why? It's 'cuz I'm so *wise*." She shot Beth a saucy grin. "We get real smart once we hit ninety. 'Fore then, we all be dumb as bricks."

"I've got a lot of years left to be as dumb as a brick, then." She thought of Will and the mess she'd made of their relationship. Every memory made her soul cry.

"You—what—twenty-three, maybe?"

"Twenty-six," Beth admitted. "I'll be twenty-seven next month."

Mrs. Hammond shook her head. "Right. You got

decades of stupidity to go. Good thing you got that nice smile and carin' heart of yours. Maybe give ya a chance of bein' forgiven for stuff."

Not much chance of that, Beth thought. Smile or no smile.

"So, what you pond'ring so hard, Beth dear?"

Beth looked into her bright, empathetic eyes and knew her thoughts and fears were in a safe harbor.

"You talked about being honest with yourself about your choices," she said. "That even when life wasn't smooth, you should do your best so you could be proud of what you'd done." Beth paused. "It was good advice. Advice I'd needed."

"I 'member that day. We was talkin' about takin' chances, too. You do anything with them words of wisdom, girl?"

She sighed. "I tried, Mrs. Hammond, but the cost was too high. The whole thing frightened me, and I knew there'd be no way I could win."

The old lady snorted. "S'not about winnin', child. Takin' chances don't count if there's no risk. If'n it's easy, if'n you can't fail sometimes, then where's the stretch? There's no challenge in that." She waggled her finger in the air at Beth. "This all 'bout a man, ain't it?"

Beth nodded.

"Then think now, what be the worst thing that could happen? He break your heart?" She shrugged. "Time mends a heart."

"What about the pain of breaking his?" Beth said. "I—I know I hurt him. I don't know how he'd ever forgive me for that."

Mrs. Hammond gave a small smile. "Now, finding that out—there's a risk where you *stretch*."

"But I don't know if I can—"

Beth was interrupted by the high-pitched jangle of the telephone. The white cordless unit was within easy reach of Mrs. Hammond's armchair.

"'Lo?" The woman's smile turned serious after a moment. She held out the phone to Beth. "S'for you, child."

"Hello?" Beth said, her heart rate speeding up at the surprise call. Who would need to reach her here?

"Beth, I'm so sorry, but I had to reach you," Jane said, her words coming out like a sob. "I'm at the hospital. Charlie's had a little accident."

CHAPTER TWELVE

Will had been up to his elbows in flu patients and high fevers when he spotted the kid. Beth's son.

He saw Lang and another med student trailing after a resident. The three of them surrounded the boy as the young doctor examined both his arm and his head abrasions. The kid seemed too calm, as though he were going into shock. And some redheaded lady—the one from the park maybe?—looked on in panic. Will figured it'd be best to step in. See if he could avert hysteria.

He handed off his latest flu case to an eager resident and strode over to the group. "Hi, miss," he said to the young woman. "I'm Dr. D—"

"You're Mommy's friend!" the kid shouted, suddenly coming to life. "Auntie Jane, I *know* him." He pointed at Will with his good arm but still winced. "Me and Mommy were at her office when he came in. And Abby gave me two lollipops that day. And Robby played garbage toss and—"

Auntie?

The woman's look of concern turned to narrow-eyed

suspicion. "You're not—I mean, are you, by chance, *Will Darcy*?"

He nodded. So Beth had talked about him to her friends and/or relatives. Huh. Well, that was something good. Maybe. He looked at the lady in front of him more closely. She didn't seem pleased by the news. Maybe name recognition wasn't such a good sign after all.

"And you are?" he asked her.

"Jane Henderson," she said. "Beth's best friend. I was watching Charlie today when he fell." She looked worried again, but this time it was entirely directed at the boy's cuts and bruises. "Is he going to be okay, Doctor?"

Will signaled Jane to hold on a minute. He dismissed the resident and the med students, but Lang asked, "May I stay and watch?" Will nodded once before turning his attention to the kid. Charlie.

The six-year-old's face was scraped bad on one side. The eyebrow gash seemed especially deep. Charlie had his left arm pressed to his chest as though it would be agony if he let it move a centimeter. A few dried tears dotted his cheeks and blood stains splattered his t-shirt. All in all, it looked as though it'd been a nasty tumble but, fortunately, nothing life threatening.

Will glanced at Beth's friend. "He'll be all right once we fix him up." He put a gentle hand on the boy's shoulder. "Listen, Charlie, I'm going to need your help to do my job. First, you'll have to tell me what happened. Then, you've got to explain every single part of your body that hurts. And, finally, you'll need to hold still while I patch you up. Think you can do all of that?"

The kid bobbed his head solemnly.

"Great," Will said, "because I keep Tootsie Pops on hand for only the bravest patients." He gave Charlie a thorough once-over just so the little boy would know he was serious. "You look like you might be one of those brave types. Is that true?"

Charlie sniffled. "Ah-huh."

"I knew it." Will carefully drew the boy's arm away from his chest, feeling for broken bones while keeping tabs on Charlie's facial expressions. The kid's eyes were red-rimmed and he clenched his jaw tight as Will pressed various places on his skin. "So, tell me about it, Charlie. How did you fall?"

Charlie sucked in some air. "I was on the top of the jungle gym being the great pirate Blackbird…I mean, Blackbeard, but my shoe slipped off and I lost my balance." His chin quivered but he didn't cry. "This hurts."

The redhead—Jane—covered her eyes. "I'm so sorry, sweetie. I should never have let you go up that high. Your mommy's going to be so angry with me."

His mommy. Beth. Will still couldn't believe it. But looking into the face of the boy, he saw little flashes of her. Not in his hair, but in his eyes. Charlie's were that same chocolaty brown. And there was something about the set of his jaw, so very stubborn.

He touched Charlie's unscratched cheek. "I know it hurts to move your arm around. Thanks for letting me examine you. I've got one more thing to do that you'll have to be extra brave for, but I'll bet you can handle it." He pointed to a room down the hall. "We're going to take a quick x-ray of your arm, okay?"

The kid nodded.

"Good." Will signaled a nurse and one of the technicians to take over this part, but the kid looked up at him with such a terrified expression that he found himself asking, "Want me to go along?"

Lang shot Will a surprised look, but Charlie and Jane

seemed grateful.

"Yes, please," Charlie whispered.

Jeez, the boy was only six and already he was the model of politeness and decorum. In this, too, Will could see Charlie's mom in him. He turned toward Jane. "I'll get a nurse to clean up the blood and the scrapes on his face. Most look like topical wounds. He didn't fall on his head did he?"

She shook her head. "Only on his arm. He got the head gashes from the poles and bars on his way down."

"All right." They walked down to x-ray. He thought about what he really wanted to ask, but saying it was hard. It carried more significance than this routine question normally would. Still, medically, he had to know. "Did you contact his mother?" he asked the woman.

"Yes. I called her a few minutes ago." She gave him an odd look that there was no way he could interpret. "She left immediately and should be here soon. Really soon."

Cripes. "That's good," he said. Maybe he'd be able to slip away before she got in. Then he wouldn't have to deal with all the emotions she brought out in him. And yet, the thought of her being in the hospital, within a few yards of him, and not getting to see her...this tore at his icy soul. Running away was pointless. He couldn't turn down an opportunity to look into her thoughtful eyes again.

When they got to the x-ray room, the boy snaked out his little fingers and tugged on Will's coat cuff. Will opened his palm and, a moment later, found Charlie's warm hand in his. Something in Will's chest began to heat up for no good reason.

They snapped the image and returned to a small exam room. Will told Lang to pull the privacy curtain shut. The nurse began wiping off the dried blood on Charlie's face while they all waited for the film to come back.

Will used the time to check in on a few other patients, though things in the ER had slowed down quite a bit, but Charlie kept drawing him back. Will found himself sneaking by, waving a little at the kid, trying to make him smile. He brought him a surgical glove that he'd blown into a balloon and was rewarded with a beamer of a grin.

Charlie was a sweet kid, but so what? This didn't change anything. Well, not much.

Okay, maybe it influenced him a little. Or a lot. If he *did* ever date Charlie's mother again, at least he didn't think the kid would kick up a big fuss about it. He might even be…excited, or something. Maybe.

When the x-ray technician got the film back to him, they took a look at it. Not a full break, but a thin fracture of the upper part of the ulna. Charlie would need a cast from elbow to wrist.

"Alrighty, Charlie. I've got some good news and some bad news," he said. "Which do you want to hear first?"

The boy squinted and Beth's friend looked all worried again. "The bad news," he said.

"Well, you're gonna need to stay brave a while longer. You have a tiny break in this part of your forearm." Will ran a finger along the length of his own ulna to demonstrate.

"Do I get to wear a cast? Is that the good news?"

Will laughed and even Jane broke a grin finally. "That's not what I was going to say but, yeah, you get to wear a cast."

"Will you sign it?" the boy asked him.

"Sure thing, kid."

"What's the other good news then?"

Will pulled out three Tootsie Pops from his doctor's

coat. "You get all of these because you're doubly—no, *triply* brave. I'm really proud of you, Charlie."

"Me, too," Jane chimed in, brushing a tear away with her sleeve.

Charlie gave him a hero-worship grin so radiant Will felt his own face glow warm.

After the cast was put on Charlie's arm, Jane stepped out into the hall to look for Beth, Lang left to follow another attending for rounds, the nurse went to refill a few supplies and Will was left alone with the boy.

What did a guy talk about with a six year old? Will rarely had problems making small talk with his young patients, but this time he was struggling. He exhaled slowly and thought of three subjects: school, television and sports. He'd hit them one at a time.

"So, how do you like school?" he asked, going for the most obvious, clichéd question ever created by adults. The kid should have rolled his eyes, but he didn't.

"Fine," Charlie said, still astoundingly polite. "I'm almost done with kindergarten. Next year I get to stay all day and have lunch there and go out for *two* recesses and everything."

"Wow. That'll be cool." Lunch? Two recesses? This was a kid's view of education, all right. Will sped ahead to the next topic. "What are your favorite TV shows?"

"Mommy doesn't let me watch a lot of TV…"

Smart Mommy.

"…but she lets me see some good DVDs and PBS Kids if it's too dark or too cold to play outside."

Will watched as Charlie poked at his hardened cast then, when he thought Will's back was turned, he sniffed at it. His little nose wrinkled and the face he made was downright comical. Will, who was studying Charlie's reflection in one of the high reflective windows, almost laughed out loud. He couldn't remember—were all kids this unintentionally funny, or was he just kind of partial to this boy?

Somebody had better come in soon, though, because he was down to his last topic. "What kinds of sports do you play, Charlie?"

The kid's face brightened. "All kinds! We do soccer and football and floor hockey in gym. That's fun. And I play basketball with Robby—"

Who the hell is Robby?

"—when I'm with Mommy at work."

Oh, that guy. Married with children. Okay. "Yeah? What else?" Will prompted, swiveling his head to see out into the hallway. When would that nurse get back?

"I love running and climbing...and playing baseball. That's my all-time favorite."

"Really? That's my all-time favorite, too." Will stopped looking for the nurse. "I loved being pitcher. What about you? What position do you like to play?"

Charlie grinned. "Catcher. But I gotta practice more. Mikey says so, too."

What was with all these other guys? "Who's Mikey?"

"My best friend at school."

Will shook his head at his own stupidity. He was getting jealous of kindergarteners. He picked up a marker and scrawled "Don't break a leg," on Charlie's cast before signing it.

"Cool," Charlie said, looking down.

"So, tell me more about Mikey."

"Mikey's got a dad, two big uncles and a bunch of cousins to play ball with. I don't have anybody," the kid said, looking a little depressed. His face wore an expression of longing Will knew only too well.

Damn. This wasn't the direction he'd wanted the

discussion to go. "How about your mom? I'll bet she plays with you sometimes."

Charlie nodded. "Yeah, but she hates baseball."

"*What?* No, that can't be true. We even went…" Then he remembered it was "Charlotte Lucas" he'd taken to the Cubs game that day. Not Beth. Never Beth. He felt a surge of anger at her, at himself and at Bingley all over again. Beth's son gave him a strange look, and he realized he'd just broken off his thought mid-sentence. "You're sure your mom doesn't like baseball? Not even a tiny bit?"

"Yep," the kid said. "She never told it to me, but I heard her say so to Auntie Jane. Twice."

"You mean, she doesn't even like the Cubs? Our Cubs?" Will said for emphasis. "She doesn't care whether or not they make it to the World Series this year? She doesn't get into watching even *their* games?"

The kid raised his palms up and shrugged dramatically, but he didn't have a chance to answer. The privacy curtain flew back and Beth rushed in toward her son.

***

"How are you, baby?" Beth said, throwing her arms around her little boy's shoulders, but taking care not to squeeze too hard. All the bandages on his head. And the *cast.* She couldn't believe something like this had happened, but she knew she couldn't blame Jane. Charlie had always been accident-prone.

"I'm okay." Her darling looked up at her with his huge brown eyes. He no doubt noticed the tears she couldn't prevent from slipping down her cheeks. "Mommy, I'm sorry I fell."

She kissed his face, trying to ignore Will's penetrating gaze across the room and Jane's concerned silence behind her. "That's okay, sweetheart. I'm only upset because I was worried about you. Does your arm hurt a lot?"

He lifted his shoulders and winced a little. "Kinda."

Finally, she raised her eyes to meet Will's. "I—um—" she started to say, but he broke in.

"Hello, Ms. Bennet. It's nice to see you again." Will's voice sounded very formal and forced. He was all doctor. All business. "Your son has a hairline fracture of the upper ulna, but the x-ray showed all other bones to be intact." He pointed to Charlie's face. "We've cleaned and bandaged the head abrasions, most of which are surface scratches and contusions. There's one wound, however, that went deeper. It's above his left eyebrow."

Beth stepped back as Will removed some rolled gauze attached with surgical tape to the spot. "Oh, honey," she whispered to Charlie as she looked at the deep gash. She grabbed her baby's hand and squeezed.

"I thought I'd give you a choice on this one. All the others should heal normally. This one will probably leave a scar unless I put in a few stitches. Three or four ought to do it, but if you'd rather not, I can try a butterfly bandage instead. That'll minimize the scarring, but not as much as the stitches would." Will looked at Charlie with a slight smile. Beth saw him wink at her son. When Charlie smiled back at him, her heart almost stopped pumping.

She swallowed. "Charlie, do you think you could let Dr. Darcy stitch up the big cut on your forehead?" Her little boy looked nervous at the mention of stitches, but he nodded anyway. "It'll be all right," she said. "He promises to do a very good job."

"Your confidence in me is inspiring," Will remarked dryly, pulling out sterilized gloves and a couple of tiny instruments.

"Well, I've seen your mother's work," she said softly.

"If you're half as good as she is, Charlie'll be just fine."

A glint of something—anger, probably—flickered across Will's face. He lifted a brow and visibly clenched his jaw. "And I'm sure you're an excellent judge of character," he said, dabbing Charlie's forehead with fresh antiseptic. "With me. With my mother. Even with Bingley. You seemed to have all of our abilities and temperaments pegged."

Well, she hadn't been trying to start a fight, but he seemed to be asking for one. His sarcasm wasn't lowering her blood pressure after today's shock, and she'd bet anything he knew that. She felt her temper rising.

"No more than you, Doctor," she said, tightly. "And, by the way, did you find anyone to get engaged to yet, or was that plan so last Wednesday?"

Will stopped prepping and glared at her.

"Holy shmoly," Jane muttered.

But, instead of answering, Will applied a topical anesthetic and, when the area was ready, began to gently stitch up Charlie's cut. He was finished in a matter of minutes.

"You're good to go," he said to Charlie, lifting him with great care off the exam table. Then, turning briefly to Beth, he added, "I'll send a nurse in here to run through everything you need to know about taking care of Charlie's cast and stitches. Someone else can do the removals, so I doubt I'll be seeing—"

"I think Charlie needs M&Ms and a soda," Jane broke in. "Why don't we go get that, and we'll find the nurse, too." She tapped Charlie's unhurt arm. "C'mon, munchkin. Let me get you a treat."

Beth watched them slip past the privacy curtain and out the door. She, too, took a step toward the hallway, but Will's voice called her back.

"So, I hear you hate baseball," he said. A touch of anger still lingered in his tone, but this time she identified something else alongside it. Hurt? Resignation? Wistfulness?

"I don't actually hate it," she admitted. "It's just...I guess I really don't understand it. All the rules and terms confuse me, and no one ever took the time to explain the game." She paused and collected her thoughts. "Look, Will, thank you for taking such good care of Charlie. I—I can't tell you how much I appreciate your being so gentle with him."

He shrugged and tossed away his plastic gloves. "It's my job."

"No, not all of it was. You were kind to him in spite of our...our history. He might've been scared to be in the hospital, but he wasn't afraid of you. That means a lot to me."

A nurse poked her head in. "Dr. Darcy? We've got trauma victims from an MVC on the Edens Expressway coming in. ETA is seven minutes."

He nodded. "Thanks. I'll be ready."

Beth glanced at the door, wishing this could have been easier. Wishing she knew what to say to this man who, under different circumstances, she'd love to throw her arms around right this second. She took a deep breath and pulled her shoulders up before facing him. "I should let you go," she said. "You'll be really busy in here soon."

"True." He paused, pinning her in place with his intense blue eyes. "Motor vehicle collisions are tough."

She'd probably never see him again unless, heaven forbid, there was another medical emergency. She'd better tell him what she wanted him to know. The censored version, anyway.

"Will, I wish you all the best. I wish I could've helped

you more with your clinic, but Bingley seemed adamant that…" She hesitated. How could she explain? Tell him that Bingley didn't think Will had a prayer of choosing to love someone like her? "…that, um, you should be the one in charge of choosing what you want or don't want. I'm just sorry for my part in our…well, you know."

A jumble of emotions flashed across his face too quickly for her to read them. He opened his mouth to speak, but a new figure appeared in the doorway. Beth's jaw dropped as she saw Bingley stride into the room. Well, speak of the devil.

"Hey, Cuz," Bingley said, raising his arm for a quick wave but keeping a healthy distance from his glowering doctor-cousin. Bingley did a double take when he recognized her, but he recovered in an instant and shot her a hasty grin. "And hello to you, too, Beth Ann Bennet. Nice seein' you again."

"Likewise," she whispered. Will still hadn't uttered a sound. He just stood there, looking between them both, his expression growing darker.

"So," Bingley said to Will, "my housekeeper said you wanted to see me?"

Will's silence was earsplitting. A tiny smile played at his lips, though, as he took a couple of steps in Bingley's direction. "You're clever," he said at last. "Maybe too clever, Bingley. It was a well-thought-out strategy to aim me in Mom's direction and then skip town for a few days. Figured I'd cool off, right?"

Bingley's eyebrows rose to his hairline and he backtracked a few paces toward the door.

Will followed him like a lion stalking his dinner. "Then showing up here, a place where you know I need to remain professional—that was also smart." He tapped his own forehead with a curved index finger and he thinned his lips. "Very, very bright dude, aren't you?"

Beth held her breath.

Bingley, meanwhile, sucked in some air. "Look, Will, like I've always told you, I had only your best—"

"Interests in mind," Will finished for him. "Yes, yes, I remember. I also remember what it feels like to be manipulated by someone who swears he loves me." He pointed at Bingley. "You have a few things to answer for."

"Ambulances pulling up," a nurse in the hallway shouted.

Bingley waved his hands in front of his chest and tried to scoot around Will. "W-we can talk later, okay? Maybe I'd, um, better get going now if you've got—"

"Thought it would be safe coming into a busy ER, eh?" Will said. "Well, think again."

Beth gasped as Will swung a fast right hook at Bingley's chin, sending the guy spinning across the exam room. Bingley slammed into a table, his arms flinging out to the sides with a crash. A large tray of medical instruments clattered onto the tiles and a worried-looking med student came rushing in.

"Is everything okay in here, Doctor?" the young man asked as he eyed the disaster on the floor and took in the sight of Bingley clutching his jaw in the corner.

"Everything is just fine, Lang." Will massaged his fist and scowled. "I'll meet you in the hall in a second."

The med student scrambled into the hallway at the sound of the gurneys rolling toward them, and Will pointed at Bingley. "You're right. We can *talk* later." His cousin had the intelligence to merely nod. Then Will turned to her. "Take care of yourself, Beth. I've got to go." His tone was strained with words left unspoken. He walked out the door and, in another moment, the frantic swim of trauma swallowed him up.

Beth held Bingley's gaze for an instant before looking down at her worn loafers. "Are you okay?"

"Yep," he said. "Kinda hoped I'd be able to avoid that particular response from him." He gave a half laugh. "Guess not."

"Do you think he'll stay mad at you for long?"

Bingley shook his head. "Will is a good guy. A great one. He's more like my kid brother than a cousin." He sighed. "And I *was* tampering in his life...a bit."

She grinned. "Just a bit."

"Yeah, well. He might not have liked my method, but he's not the type to hold a grudge. Even after something like this. He ever tell you about the time I rescued him from the lizard trapped in his sleeping bag?"

She thought back to when she and Will were at the baseball game. She remembered how he'd joked about Bingley and a lizard. "This was the night you two were camping out in his backyard, right?"

"Right." Bingley traced his bruised jaw with his thumb. "What he probably didn't mention was that I was the one who'd put Mr. Lizard in his sleeping bag."

She covered her mouth with her hand to trap a giggle. "What?"

He nodded. "It's true. I put it in there to scare him, but then I also wanted to be the one to come to his rescue. Will guessed right away what I was doing, but he let me pretend to be heroic for a while." He gave her arm a quick and friendly squeeze. "It's a type of pattern we've established. See, up until that night, he was afraid of reptiles. I showed him they're not so scary."

Beth was starting to understand. "And what did he do to you in response?"

He tapped his stomach. "I was justly rewarded with a

major slug to the gut." He winked. "But, then again, I was still his cousin and his best friend. And I was the only kid he invited to his eleventh birthday party a few weeks later." He glanced around at the mess they'd created then righted a box of bandages on the table nearby. He tossed her a handful of cotton balls and a wry smile. "It's not easy being Will's Catalyst for Change, but somebody's gotta do it, eh?"

He ambled out of the exam room with a parting wave, while she stood in place, squishing one of the cotton balls between her fingers. It had been a day that inspired questions. Mrs. Hammond's. Charlie's. Bingley's. Will's, too. And her own most pressing point of curiosity: Did Will consider women with children more or less frightening than panicky reptiles?

All in all, she'd put what little money she had on the lizard being the preferred companion.

CHAPTER THIRTEEN

The crash victim Will was working on, a young husband and father, stabilized within minutes, so he had a spare second to glance through the window and watch Beth walking away. Her friend was by her side. Her son was clutching her hand. It was all he could do not to throw his sterilized mask on the ground and sprint after her.

But of course he didn't.

Hypocritical of him, wasn't it, implying that Bingley was a coward? That Beth was a liar? That his own anger was justifiable and totally logical?

He thought of his mom. In her own way, she'd been trying to manipulate him into a relationship for years. Just like Bingley. Why wouldn't he blame her for some of this? Rationally he knew she was just as much—if not more— at fault than Bingley. But he knew something else about her, too. He knew there was a passion in her. One directed at protecting him and loving him like no one else in the world ever would or could.

There was something about the power of a mother's

love. He knew she'd never purposely do anything to hurt him. That his real and true *best interests* were in each beat of her heart, in every breath she took and in any action she initiated.

He'd seen that same kind of fierce love in Beth's eyes when she held and comforted her son. He could sense it through the glass windows and across the courtyard as they left the hospital.

He had been acting like a coward because he was afraid to feel emotions of that intensity toward anyone. And then acting like a liar because he'd spent several weeks denying his need for that very thing.

He leaned out into the hallway, peering down the length of it in search of Lang. Will spotted him with his back up against a support beam and his fingers steepled together.

Fresh grief washed over the guy's face. Lang's patient, the wife and mother, must not have fared as well as Will's patient. But Lang seemed to be working hard to keep his sentiments in check. A part of Will was proud of him. Another part ached for the loss. The loss of Lang's full range of emotion and natural compassion... before the job forcibly tempered it.

And where had *his* full range of emotion gone?

Will looked at the unconscious man on the bed in front of him. His vitals were normal. The injuries he incurred would most likely heal. But what would happen to this man's young family? How would he and his two children recover from the loss of the central woman in their lives?

To his horror, Will felt tears prick his eyes. He jabbed at them with his cuff as he might if he were wiping sweat from his face. It didn't work. They kept returning, the damned things. He had to get out of this room.

At the first opportunity, Will slipped away. He hid in his office, locked the door and let all the pain he'd been holding back crash over him. Then, for a long while, he thought about what his mom said. Did the important things line up between him and Beth? Were the rest just details that could be worked through? In his opinion, yes.

He also thought about what parents give up for their children...how their lives change in an instant and, yet, how their relationships also grow into something more precious than words could express.

How could he explain his admiration and devotion toward his mom? How could he quantify Beth's love for her son? There were a million things these days he couldn't seem to put into words. But there were a few he could.

He switched on his computer, logged on to his email account and clicked on COMPOSE.

What to type? Maybe something simple like...*Hi there, Beth. Long time, no email.*

No. Too flippant.

Or maybe, *We have some unfinished business, Beth. Can we get together and discuss a few things?*

Definitely, no. Too cold. Too rational.

Or he could just be honest and write, *Beth, it was unbelievably hard seeing you here in the ER today. To have you so near and, yet, not be able to hug you or tell you how much I've missed your company—it was painful. You've got me rethinking everything. Being with you on our few dates gave me something wonderful to look forward to and, despite all that happened, I miss that.*

Hell, no. He didn't need to sound like a ridiculous greeting card. Even if the words were true.

He sighed loudly, touched his fingers to the keyboard and tried again.

Beth, I'd like it if we could talk. Would you be willing to meet me at the Koffee Haus sometime this weekend? Please let me know. I hope Charlie's recovery is going smoothly. Best wishes to you both.—Will.

He read it over twice then hit SEND.

***

Bingley was waiting for him in the cafeteria an hour later.

"What now?" Will said, none too politely.

His cousin stroked the darkening bruise near his chin, and Will felt a surge of guilt. Then he remembered his cousin's interfering behavior. He clenched his jaw.

"You really love her, eh?" Bingley said.

"Yes, you meddling fool. I told you so before. Please, would you stop playing stupid games for five minutes? I need some coffee."

"Oh, they're not so stupid, Cuz," Bingley said, handing him a tall Mocha Java in a Koffee Haus cup. Still hot. "You may have had a reason to punch me today, I'll concede, but you didn't let me explain where I was these past few days."

"Okay, I'll play along one last time. Where were you?"

"Europe."

Will froze. "Why? Are your parents okay?"

"Yep. Popped over there to wish Mom a Happy Mother's Day in Florence. Ate a big piece of birthday tiramisu. Got it all in just under the wire Sunday. Then I headed north across the border. Wanted to authorize in person a very large withdrawal from one of my Swiss accounts."

Will eyed the paper his cousin pulled out from his breast pocket. It couldn't be. But, from the smug look on Bingley's face, it was. "You're funding the clinic?"

"Smart guy, aren't you?" He handed Will the paper.

"This is a copy of the transfer of cash from my account to one I set up for the clinic."

Will swallowed and read the banker-speak on the page. "Much as I appreciate this, I've gotta ask…why? I didn't get in the five dates before your birthday. Why did you change your mind?"

Bingley rolled his eyes. "For someone with such a big brain, you can be a real dummy. I never cared about the number of dates, Cuz. I only cared where your heart was in the middle of this mess. When you admitted you loved her, that was all I needed to know."

"Oh." Will couldn't think of another word at that moment.

"But tell me," his cousin said with a wicked twinkle in his eye, "do you think she loves you back?"

***

Beth studied Will's message, reading it not once, not twice, but a full fifteen times before it registered. Could he actually want to see her again…after everything? Impossible. But there it was, documented in cyber text, with a printable hardcopy of the words he'd sent just a click away.

She typed, *Saturday. Ten a.m.* and sent it. Then she slumped in her chair.

She doubted his interest in meeting her had anything at all to do with getting back together romantically. He probably just had some residual anger he wanted to get off his chest.

Fair enough.

It was one of those events she needed to be present at. Something she'd done that she'd have to take responsibility for. What was it Mrs. Hammond had said? That she should face the choices she'd made and didn't make… Beth's choices had led her to this moment. She needed to be a grownup and do the right thing. Let Will have his say tomorrow. She owed him that.

The next day couldn't come too quickly. They met at the agreed upon time and, when she first spotted him, she drew in an anxious breath. The smell of fresh-brewed coffee had never been so nauseating.

"Hello, Will," she managed.

His forehead creased and his lips tightened. "Beth. Hi, there." He motioned toward a table. "What can I get you? A Kenyan? A Kona? Something else?"

She began to shake her head and was about to say, *Nothing, thanks*—but then she realized she wouldn't have anything to do with her hands if she refused. "Anything," she said instead. "Whatever you think is different or unusually good."

An odd light sprang into his eyes. Approval? She didn't bother trying to figure it out. He might be glad she was being more adventurous in her coffee drinking, but he hardly approved of her on a personal level. He'd lost the bet and the funding for the clinic because he couldn't bring himself to ask her out a fifth time. Not once he knew who she really was. At least, not until today.

"Be right back," he said. And sure enough, a few minutes of heart-pounding solitude later, he returned with two steaming grande mugs. "Amaretto Cherry. Decaf. It's considered the 'Sweethearts' Flavor of the Month."

He said this without sarcasm. She eyed him sharply. He said this without rolling his eyes or scowling. What was going on here?

"Um, thanks," she murmured, sniffing it. Even her rebellious stomach didn't seem to mind this one. "Smells great."

He plopped a bag of oatmeal-raisin cookies on the table in front of her and sat down. This was so reminiscent of their first date she almost cried.

Instead, she took a cautious sip.

"So, how's your research paper coming along?" he asked.

She choked on her coffee. "What?"

He wore a straight face. No hint of mockery. "The research project you were working on. Finished yet?"

"W-well, yes."

The corners of his lips tilted precariously upward. He couldn't possibly be smiling...could he?

"How did I do?" he said. "All in all, did I provide enough information for your sociology experiment?"

Okay. *Now* there was an edge of something more dangerous in his tone. "I—I tried to be completely fair in my evaluation. I'd been looking at gender-role stereotypes and—" She paused. "Why are we talking about this? You can't possibly want to know the details of my study."

"Sure I can. It was, after all, what brought you to me in the first place. Your reason for our paths crossing."

She looked down at her coffee and fingered the smooth rim. "Will, pretending to be someone else to gather research for my class was wrong. Truly wrong. But not only for the obvious reasons. Putting false personal data on the Love Match website was clearly not me at my most candid. Lying to your face wasn't especially ethical either. But I also lied to myself. A part of me really wanted to *be* Charlotte Lucas for a while. A part of me wanted to be the kind of woman a man like you would've been interested in."

She got up to leave. She knew her eyes couldn't keep the tears from flowing for long, and she had to get out of there soon. Very soon.

"Sit down, Beth. We're not through talking yet. At least—" He gave her a guarded look. "At least I'm not through." He paused again and nodded toward her chair. "Please."

She exhaled slowly and returned to her seat, snatching a Koffee Haus napkin from the table and crushing it.

"Thank you," he said.

Beth took a long, hot gulp of Amaretto Cherry and searched the room for any excuse to break eye contact with Will. She spotted the sugar packets on the table, grabbed one and made a production of tearing it open and stirring its contents into her drink.

"Cookie?" he asked.

Another possible fidgeting object. Just what she needed. "Yes, please."

He held open the plastic bag. "So, how's Charlie doing? His arm? His face? Are the cast and stitches getting on his nerves yet?"

She reached into the bag. At any other time she would've laughed at the normalcy of their conversation and their actions. Bystanders might think they were Just Another Couple—eating, drinking, chatting. They'd be wrong.

"No," she said, biting into a cookie that rivaled one of Grandma Kate's and striving to keep her voice steady. "So far he still sees them as honor badges. His best friend Mikey stopped by last night to bring over a get-well card and to sign the cast. He treated Charlie like a celebrity."

"And what about you? Have you recovered from the shock of it all?"

"Of Charlie being rushed to the ER? Oh, no. I imagine it'll be months before I stop having nightmares about it. As it is, I'm pretty sure it took five years off my life."

She listened to herself playing this small-talk charade with Will and very nearly rolled her eyes. She wished he'd get to the point and say what he needed to say. She wanted them to stop making sport of this discussion. It required more endurance than a marathon...or a Cubs doubleheader. But Will, it seemed, had no intention of putting her out of her misery anytime soon, and she was at a loss for a way to get him to move things along.

"Charlie was an incredibly stoic patient for a six year old. I was impressed," he said.

"Thanks." She hesitated. "Look, about all that. Thank you for treating him so kindly when he was at the hospital and for the way—"

"You already thanked me yesterday. I'm glad I could be there to help." He stopped, pinged his fingernail against his coffee cup and then shoved the half-full mug away from him. "Why did you decide to meet me here today, Beth?"

She almost laughed. This was the guy who'd accused *her* of asking too many peculiar questions. "I'm not sure what you mean. I met you because you asked me to."

"No, I know. I meant, seriously, why did you agree to it? What were the reasons you gave yourself for coming?"

She put down what was left of her cookie. "Well, I felt I owed you that much. You said you wanted to talk, and I thought it was a fair request."

His lips thinned to razor-sharp lines. "So, your being here has to do with acting equitably and paying off a type of emotional debt." He closed his eyes. "And when you got up to leave a few minutes ago, did you imagine you'd already accomplished that goal?"

She tossed her crinkled napkin on the table. "I don't know what you want from me, Will. I came because you asked me to. I stayed for the same reason. If I didn't respect you and greatly care about your feelings, I wouldn't be sitting here still. I guess I shouldn't be anymore." She pushed her chair back and got to her feet. "I've apologized over and over, but I can't make you forgive me. If you don't, you don't. I have no choice but to accept that."

"Not so fast, Beth."

What now? "You can't keep calling me back while at the same time pushing me away. Thanks for the coffee, but I—"

"You apologized, but I didn't." He put his head in his palms and rocked slowly in place. Right there at the table. Beth glanced around but nobody seemed to be watching them. For the second time in five minutes, she sat back down, across from him, and she tried to understand what was happening here.

"What are you talking about?" she said.

"I haven't had a chance yet to apologize to *you.*" He whispered these words but they were crystal clear. A loudspeaker couldn't have announced his intentions more dramatically. He wanted to say he was sorry?

"What for?" she said before realizing he was probably talking about the bet. "Look, if this is about Bingley's—"

"For waiting this long," he interrupted her, "to admit aloud to you, and to myself, that I've fallen in love with you." He met her gaze and held it.

She pushed both her coffee and her cookie away and blinked. If other people were talking in the room, she could no longer hear them. If a light breeze from Lake Michigan blew by, she'd topple over. If someone asked if she could feel her legs, she wouldn't be able to reply because, A, she couldn't feel any physical sensations at all aside from the hammering of her heart and, B, she also couldn't speak to save her life.

Fortunately, Will didn't require an immediate response.

"I fell in love with you twice. When you were 'Charlotte' I loved your energy, your intelligence, the three million questions you asked, the way you charmed my mother, your beauty and the fact that every time I thought about you I smiled."

He paused. She managed a small nod of acknowledgment.

"When I realized you were 'Beth' I loved all those 'Charlotte' things plus the devotion you showed to your son and the kindness you showed to my crazy, well-intentioned cousin and the loyalty you showed to your friend Jane and the dedication you showed toward your job. Any chance I could get a few of those qualities directed toward me?"

She recovered a teensy part of her voice. "But I thought...I, um, I—" Then a realization hit her. "Oh, wait. This is about the clinic somehow, isn't it? You got Bingley to extend the deadline, maybe, or to—"

"No. I don't have any outside conditions that need to be satisfied. I asked you here because I wanted to be with you. Bingley did come back to see me, that's true, but it wasn't until after I'd sent you that last email asking for this meeting."

Then he explained, to her growing surprise, how Bingley gave him the money anyway, just based on Will's feelings for her. "So, this is not about some juvenile bet. It's not about the clinic in any way. It's not about anything outside of the two of us, Beth. It's about only us. Together."

"R-really?"

"Yes, really. But I don't actually know where I stand on this one at all. You seemed to like me when you were Charlotte Lucas, but this woman...Beth Bennet...I don't know what she thinks."

When sensation began to rush back into her body, it started with her head. Tears she'd hoped would stay at bay began pooling in her eyes. She forced them back and swallowed. "Will, certain essential things about me haven't changed. I'm still planning on being a social worker—"

"I know. Dan told me. And you're not the one assigned to be my consultant for the clinic. I know that, too."

"So, what then? You don't have a problem with my occupation now?"

He shook his head, but very slightly. "In my opinion, a social worker trained under Dan Noelen is of a special breed. It'll probably take me some time to accept that social workers in general are not the evil beings I once thought they were. It's an emotional not rational impulse, deep-seated from childhood. But Dan's earned my respect and so have you. I guess, one person at a time, I'm learning to see your profession differently."

Her heart began to flutter around in her chest. She'd earned his respect? "But how can you discount the lies I told you? They were the kind of lies you despised the most. Lies about my essential self." She stared at him, trying to see into his soul and not sure if what she was reading was his affection or just her wishful thinking reflected back. "You've forgiven me then?"

He reached across the tiny table and grasped her hands. "Yes, Beth. What I'm asking, though, here and now, is if you've forgiven *me*. I lied to you, too. My motives for getting on the Lady Catherine site weren't pure either, even though I genuinely liked you once we met face to face." He squeezed her fingers tighter. "You were right when you said there was no such thing as degrees of lying. Regardless of my reasons for doing it, the result was the same. I wasn't truthful with you…but now I want to be."

The love she felt for this man, all the feelings of warmth and happiness, began to swell inside her heart. She smiled at him, trying to pour every one of those delectable emotions into it. He smiled back, happiness lighting up his face.

"Of course I forgive you…" She paused, though, as the rest of their conflict came rushing back to her. "Oh."

"What's the 'Oh' for?"

"Charlie."

Will's blue eyes met her brown ones. "I hadn't forgotten you have a son."

"But would you be prepared to be a part of his life? Would you let him into yours?" Speaking became a struggle, but she continued, "I remember you said you didn't ever want to be involved with single mothers. And you didn't want the pressure of being put in that—how did you explain it? That 'B team' role."

"Something you need to understand, Beth. I'm not always consistent or predictable. Changing my mind is not impossible." He threw her a small grin as if his latest statement were news to her.

"Perhaps not, but jumping into Charlie's world and welcoming him into yours isn't an activity that can be chosen lightly or be easily discarded."

"I wouldn't be taking it lightly," he replied. "And I'm not planning on doing any discarding."

She looked at him, pretty sure her facial expression revealed as much wariness as she felt. "Will—"

He held up a hand to stop her. "No. You're not listening here. Not that I blame you for being skeptical, but something happened to me this spring. Something you caused." He brought her palm to his chest. "Feel my heart. It's beating wildly." And, sure enough, she could feel it pounding away under his shirt. "This is because of my boundless affection for you... and because of the hopefulness that fills me whenever I'm around Charlie."

He lifted her fingers to his lips and kissed each knuckle. Her breath caught, and all she could think of was how much she wanted to push this silly table out of the way so they could really embrace. He leaned over and touched the tip of her nose with his puckered mouth. All of her went tingly.

He grinned. The light of his joy reached his eyes and sparkled out at her. "Before I knew about Bingley's check," he said, "and even before I knew about Beth Bennet's real life, my heart had chosen you. And once I met Charlie, sweetheart, my heart chose him, too."

She couldn't believe what she was hearing. "You mean from that day you walked into Social Services and saw 'Charlotte Lucas' there...with her son? I—I just can't figure how—"

"You're trying to be too logical and too rational. This is one of those emotional, intuitive kinds of things. Hey, I thought women were supposed to be the experts in that?" He raised a mocking eyebrow at her.

She shrugged and waved a white napkin in surrender.

He snatched it from her hand, paused, then waved it back. "Look, Charlie tugged at my heartstrings. To be honest, I didn't want to like him, but I did. He made me see, especially in the ER yesterday, that all stepfather-like relationships don't have to be the way I'd experienced them growing up. That's what I meant by feeling hope. I feel something wonderful emerging between us. Between Charlie and me. And I'd be willing to bet some of that has to do with our mutual love for you."

She sniffled but had long ago given up on trying to

rein in those tears. "Haven't you learned yet not to make bets?" she said. Love, the anti-gravity force that it was, tugged the corners of her lips upward.

He laughed and gently dabbed her face with the edge of her confiscated napkin. "You know," he said, "Bingley put me on the spot this week. He asked which caused me more pain—you or the millions I thought I'd lost. I have great dreams for the clinic and for what a bundle of money can do, but all I could think about in that moment was you, Beth. Missing you, above all else, is what's been keeping me up at night."

The heck with the table. She stood up and slid it to the side so she could reach him faster. Her arms wrapped around his waist and slowly, wonderfully she felt his arms encompassing all of her as well. Sighing, she squeezed tighter and felt him respond in kind.

Then his lips touched hers in the most heartening of kisses, warm and uplifting and loving. Like a film soundtrack in the background, someone in the coffee shop hummed "Here Comes the Bride," while others applauded.

"I guess that's my cue to get down on one knee and propose," Will said.

"You planned to?"

"Well, I didn't bring the ring along, although I've kinda got one picked out," he said, grinning sheepishly. "I guess I just didn't want to be overconfident. And, also, I figured you might like some time to get Charlie used to the changes coming up in his life. Once that cast comes off, he and I have got some major pitching and catching sessions to get started on…and Cubs games to go to…and you and I have some new siblings to create for him…and—"

"*What?*" she said.

He kissed her again. "Maybe I'm getting a little ahead of myself. All I'm saying is—we can work this out—if you're willing to risk it." His eyes gazed deeply into hers. "Are you, Beth? Are you willing to take a chance on us?"

Through her tears she grinned at him. "You can bet on it."

***

The next day, a few hours before her long-awaited graduation, Beth stopped at the university library to return a couple of books and to say a nostalgic goodbye to one of her favorite college haunts. She logged onto a computer to check her email and saw "Sender: Will Darcy." The message line read: "Number 49 Rewrites Profile."

She clicked on it, of course. The permanent grin she wore today only broadened at the thought of "Her Man" staying up late to type this. He wrote:

To the Lady of my Heart, I seek someone with very specific qualities.

First, she must have light-brown hair. I especially like long wild curls. And I insist upon a woman with chocolaty-brown eyes. No other color will do.

Second, she must be passionate about her profession and be the kind of person who knows how to care for young and old alike. A social worker might be just the right career choice, in fact.

Third, she must like coffee and cookies and movies and popcorn, but she absolutely should not like camping…although I'll try to persuade her otherwise. A double sleeping bag in a tent can be really cozy when shared with someone other than a lizard. And, while I'd like to make a Cubs convert out of her, if she wrinkles up her cute nose at the thought of baseball games, I'll still love her dearly.

Fourth, she needs to be intelligent, loyal, compassionate and hardworking. I'd especially like it if The Woman Destined For Me possessed these traits.

And, last but far from least, she must be mother to a bright and adorable six-year-old boy. This is a firm requirement.

Do you qualify? If yes, and only if yes, please respond promptly. I've been waiting my whole life for you.

Your Hopeful Perfect Match.

Beth hit the REPLY key.

I've been waiting all my life for you, Dear Sir, she typed. *Consider me yours. With love and hugs from me and best wishes from Lady Catherine.*

She pressed SEND, logged off and said a fond farewell to the life she was leaving behind. Then she immediately headed home to embrace her new one.

STORY EXCERPTS
FROM THREE OF MARILYN BRANT'S
CONTEMPORARY ROMANCES

On Any Given Sundae

In this light romantic comedy involving a shy dessert cookbook writer and a former football star, we're taken to an ice cream parlor in small-town Wisconsin where two people who couldn't be more different from each other find themselves falling in love...

Elizabeth rarely swore aloud but, in her mind, she was cursing not just a blue streak, but also a red, orange, yellow and green streak. She was, in fact, well on her way to a complete blasphemous rainbow, and Rob Gabinarri hadn't even arrived yet.

Of all people. She never thought she'd have to make it through so much as a ten-minute soda pop break with *him* again. The boy who'd broken her heart and didn't even know it.

Or maybe he did know it.

She couldn't decide which was the greater tragedy.

A snazzy red Porsche convertible squealed to a stop behind her sensible blue Toyota Camry, and the town's Golden Boy stepped out of the car and into the empty confectionary shop.

"Hey, Lizzy. Long time, no see," he said, glancing around the shop in a frantic kind of way.

"E-Elizabeth," she corrected automatically.

"Oh, all right. Sorry."

She stared at him, which of course he didn't notice because he was too busy looking at everything else in the place besides her.

He walked into the backroom then out of it again.

He peered into the washrooms.

He opened and shut a few closets.

He paced back and forth, sat down in a booth, got back up and paced some more.

The guy was as tall and muscular and breathtaking as he'd been a decade before when he used to saunter through the unremarkable halls of Wilmington Bay High School, oblivious to anyone and anything beyond the football field and his bevy of admirers. If it were possible, he seemed even more youthful and in command now than he did at age eighteen.

And she felt about as queasy as she'd felt the last time they'd been face to face.

Finally, his pacing stopped. "Where is my uncle?" he asked in a husky whisper, directing the query at a tray of chocolate-dipped sugar cookies. "Uncle?" he called out. "Uncle Pauly?"

She wanted to tell him, but the words were lodged in her esophagus and, anyway, he wasn't talking to her.

He strode into the backroom again, as if convinced the elderly Italian man could be found hiding behind a jar of candied cherries or a vat of butterscotch syrup. The long black eyelashes blinked in confusion when he emerged into the main shop once again, his gaze and those nutmeg-brown eyes directed at her.

"Don't tell me he left already." This was more a threat than a question. He shook his head at her as though that gesture alone would discourage an affirmative reply.

She held her breath and nodded.

"*Where* is he?"

She pursed her lips, just as she'd learned in her special speech tutorials so long ago, formed the first letter and tried to push it out of her mouth. But she stuttered anyway.

"L-Lufthansa. F-Fl-Flight four-oh-three."

He cocked his gorgeous head to one side and stared at her in the way she'd grown so accustomed to during her miserable school years: *Poor Old Lizzy*, the look said. *What a geeky dweeb.*

"What time is it scheduled to depart?" he asked her with an affected gentleness that made her want to rip out his vocal cords.

She tapped her watch and gathered her courage for whatever might happen next. "T-Twenty m-m-minutes a-ago."

"Oh, bloody hellfire!" Rob shouted, adding several inventive phrases to his curse before pausing to take a breath.

Elizabeth had managed to squeeze out a few additional syllables of explanation, but Rob was quick to catch on to the full meaning, she noticed, even when words were left unspoken.

"Uncle Pauly said he'd be gone only a couple of weeks." He rubbed his palms against his eyes. "Not a freaking *month*. And he never mentioned *Europe*." He pounded his fist on the ice-cream-window part of the counter three times in rapid succession. "He said everything would be explained when I got up here." He turned toward her. "Guess you were elected to supply the details."

If she'd been capable of it, she would've laughed. Oh, yeah. Now that was a first. One for the record books. Elizabeth Daniels: Verbal Disseminator of Information. Hee-hee. Ha-ha.

"S-Sorry," she said.

He paused. "I didn't mean it like that. I'm just..." But words must have defied him, too because he left the sentence uncompleted.

A jangling of bells broke the silence.

"Howdy, folks," the chatty old florist from down the block said. "Hey, Pauly, Siegfried," he called. "Need to get me a double scoop of Cherry-Almond S—" He stopped mid-speech and surveyed Rob from the top of his dark Italian head right down to his pricey black-and-white Nikes. "Holy Hydrangea. Is that really Roberto Gabinarri standing in front of me?"

Rob grinned but a look of something other than gratification (wariness, perhaps?) slid over his face like a well-formed mask. "Good to see you again, sir. You're looking fit as ever."

The gentleman shook his head as if disbelieving the sight. "Been blazing a hot trail through Chicago, I hear. But, we've all missed you in Wilmington Bay, son. Does your uncle know you're back?" He didn't wait for Rob to answer. "Pauly! Siegfried!" He raised his palms. "Where are they?"

She watched Rob inhale several slow breaths. She could almost see him selecting his words with precision, the way a pastry chef might chose just the right filling for a pie.

"They're taking a much-deserved vacation," he said, nodding sagely at the older gentleman and motioning him closer as if letting him in on a deep family secret. "And we couldn't let them close the shop now, could we? During June?"

The florist's eyes grew large. "Oh, no."

"Of course not. Especially since their best customers were counting on them." Rob winked at the man and grabbed an ice cream scoop. "This cone's on the house," he said, digging into the tub of Cherry-Almond Swirl and piling the sweet concoction in massive, if inexpert, blobs atop a sugar cone. "Uncle Pauly's orders."

So Rob was going to start bribing and spin-doctoring, was he? Fine. She'd play along. In fact, she had to hand it to him. Considering the look of bliss on the talkative florist's face, the gossip he'd inevitably spread about them could only be in their favor. She clamped her mouth shut and did her part by passing the man a paper napkin and shooting him a closed-lipped smile.

"Why, thank you, dearie," the florist said to her. "Gotta get back to talking to my geraniums and begonias before they start complaining." He licked his cone and twinkled his delight at her with his eyes.

She waved him off without uttering a sound, a trick she'd perfected through years of social avoidance, then she grabbed her notebook and ripped out the page she'd been working on. She handed it to Rob.

"What's this?" he said, slumping against the counter.

With her pen, she pointed to the heading she'd written in block letters.

"A schedule? For what? The shop?" He stared at her as if this were the most foreign of concepts.

She nodded.

"For us? To divide up the opening and closing times?"

Good. He could read. She nodded again.

"But who's going to work the shifts in between? Last time I talked with Uncle Pauly, he said he and Siegfried were doing most of the serving themselves. Said they didn't trust many people and they'd only hire out part-time helpers during really busy times or when one of them was sick."

She knew this, which was why she'd have to rely more heavily on Jacques, and why she'd called both Gretchen and Nick and told them they absolutely *had* to come over tomorrow to help her with this. She was desperate.

"M-M-My fr-friends will be w-working here," she said.

"Well, great," he said, looking relieved. "Hey, I mean, if you think you can handle all of the organizing, get trustworthy people to take the over shifts and all, you can count on me to chip in with other things. Funding their salaries for the month. Doing all the stock ordering. Sending out publicity notices. Anything you need, just so I can be back in Chicago soon."

She winced. She'd been especially dreading relaying this part of Pauly's parting message. Although she didn't know the precise reason, she sensed Rob wouldn't like the news. "Y-You can't l-leave."

"Why not?" he said, but the uneasiness in his tone convinced her he wasn't surprised there might be a complication.

"P-Pauly called your m-m-mother. T-Told her to expect you for Sunday d-d-dinner tonight. And every n-night."

"Oh, hell."

She pushed her long, unruly hair out of her eyes and blinked at him. Funny, she'd never before seen the Golden Boy's rugged olive complexion look quite so peaked.

"Lizzy," he said, setting her carefully constructed schedule back on the counter. "You're looking at a dead man."

And with that, he collapsed into a six-foot heap of hunky male onto the floor.

Double Dipping

Opposites collide in this light mystery/romantic comedy when a dedicated 2nd grade teacher fights the school's new financial director in order to reinstate a much-beloved autumn festival. But secrets, ambition, attraction and meddling family members complicate matters in this small Midwestern town...

Garrett watched the curvaceous blonde throw a few last things together, and he shook his head behind her back. This was exactly the kind of individual who could get away with skimming budget funds if she wanted to. No one would suspect someone as lovely and as, well, *wholesome-looking* as Cait Walsh. Not of fiscal misdeeds.

Still, it would be bad form to deny a teacher her glitter. The school board had approved the office supplies change, but he wondered who'd orchestrated it and why. Something seriously strange was afoot in this district.

He studied Cait. She was young, dynamic and closer to his sister's age than his. Twenty-five, maybe. But unlike Sis, this shapely woman was a neat freak who used round vowel tones as weapons. She challenged him with that reserved posture, that combination of clarity and caution.

With those huge gray-green eyes, freckle-splattered nose and forehead creased in concentration over God knew what, she was cute as hell.

Which annoyed him. He had too much to do. A leak to pinpoint. He had no intention of finding *anyone* "cute as hell." Least of all a potential embezzler from Wisconsin.

He saw her lift a bulky beige tote with the letters "CLW" stitched in green. It looked as heavy as a golf bag, but shorter and twice as dense. She had it crammed with papers, scratch 'n' sniff stickers, lots of stuff he couldn't see. He'd have offered to carry it for her, but she grabbed it tight. Didn't look like she'd trust the FBI with that thing. Huh. Suspect behavior.

"What's the 'L' stand for?" He pointed to her monogram. "It wouldn't be Lynn, would it?" He squinted. "Leigh? Or Loretta?"

"None of the above." Cait locked her classroom door.

Then again, maybe secrecy was just part and parcel of being a woman. They always thought they had to be so mysterious.

"So, what? You're not going to tell me? Think I'll laugh?"

She nodded, standing still and staring at him in the hallway.

He puffed out some hot air. He'd have to brush up on his chitchatting. Not a good idea to alienate the staff so soon, even if he had suspicions about somebody. He'd known her for…what? A whole fifteen minutes? And already she pretty clearly despised him. Well, never let it be said he couldn't make a strong first impression.

"I won't laugh." He tried to radiate sincerity.

She gave him a thorough once-over. "Livie," she

mumbled. "After my grandmother Olivia."

"Oh." He shrugged. "That's not so bad. Olivia's nice, too. Why'd your parents shorten it?"

At this she chuckled. "Think about it, Mr. Ellis. You couldn't have grown up around here. Even in Wisconsin—the 'Dairy State'—having the initials C.O.W. is hardly a woman's deepest desire."

A laugh erupted from deep within him. So there was a sense of humor behind the snow queen façade. Good. Maybe she'd thaw a bit, they could talk, he'd figure out her angle and, hopefully, discount her from his investigation. He needed to concentrate on forwarding his career…and on keeping his father from disowning him. Ogling attractive women was his brother's department, not his.

"You have bright parents," he said finally. "Bet you appreciated their foresight."

"I did." She surprised him with a grin that lit up her whole face. For a moment he was rendered speechless.

They strolled outside toward the parking lot.

"Okay," she said. "Now that you know my secret, what's *your* middle name?"

Sheesh. He hadn't been thinking. Sharing his middle name could only land him in boiling water. "Mine's not real interesting."

The light in her face vanished. She turned huge, distrustful eyes on him. "So?"

He grimaced. "My middle initial's 'M,' how 'bout you guess?"

"What? I practically told you mine outright. There's no reason to hedge with me. It couldn't be *that* terrible."

"Oh, don't be so sure. Your parents altered yours from your namesake's to be less embarrassing, my parents did nothing of the kind." He hesitated, praying she'd back off. The name recognition, he knew from years of painful experience, could be instantaneous.

But no such luck. This Miss Walsh was a persistent one.

Her forehead crinkled. "Hmm. Well, it couldn't be Michael or Matthew, could it? Those aren't unusual enough to upset anyone. Max, maybe? What about Mitch? Or, Marvin?"

"I wish," he muttered. And he did. For maybe the ninety-thousandth time he wished he came from a family that wasn't internationally famous.

They reached their vehicles, and he changed the subject. "Look," he told her, "why don't you jump in with me? It'll be easier than taking two cars. I can drive you back here later."

"Oh, um…sure."

He opened the passenger door of his red BMW and held it for her. She slid into the black leather seat, her eyes bulging at the rows of gadgets on the dash. He knew how impressive it looked. He liked his cars complicated, his women simple. Yet another reason the chilly and changeable Miss Walsh posed a problem: She did *not* seem simple. But someone was meddling with funds and, although instinct and experience told him Cait didn't have the bearing of a ringleader, she might know who was at the center of these thefts.

He slipped into the driver's seat and retrieved a second list from the glove compartment. Time for a test.

He pasted on a grin, wondering how invested she was in this silly fall festival. If he could draw her off track, it might not be much. "Now that we're out of school, I hope you don't mind one addition to our plans. I need to grab a few things from the bookstore before they close. Is it okay if we head there first?"

She gave a curt nod and laced her fingers together, looking about as enthusiastic as a shop mannequin.

Within ten minutes, he had them parked in front of Bookends. First they'd book shop, then they'd drive to the supplies store. His two-part strategy to relax, converse, slide into informality. He'd try to find out what she knew, if anything. If he could rule her out, he could get back to investigating the problem. Alone.

Garrett leaped out of the car. "You coming in?" he asked as she sat, pensive, in the passenger's seat.

"No, I'll just wait here for you."

Damn. "Are you sure? If you don't want to browse, there's a nice coffee bar and snack area inside. You could relax a little."

She glared at him like he'd suggested a round of strip poker. "I'm fine here. *Really*. Get what you need. Take your time."

"Okay." What could he do? Garrett tossed her his car keys. "If you want music, feel free to pop something in. CDs are in a case under your seat." At that she looked almost intrigued.

"Thank you." Cait doled out one of her angelic smiles. It made him tense, uncomfortable and kind of…warm. Aw, hell.

He took a few brisk strides across the street toward the shop. He had a job to do, he reminded himself again. He didn't need complications like, oh, lady swindlers.

But he hoped to heaven she was innocent and he could maintain a friendly distance from her. Something about this woman just got to him. A point underscored by the fact that, as he entered the bookstore, he found himself wondering what he might buy her to make her smile again.

At him. Like that.

Holiday Man

In this romance told over a year of holidays, a small-town girl who runs a holiday-themed inn up in scenic Door County meets a wealthy Minneapolis businessman one snowy winter's evening. The sparks they create succeed in heating up the chilly Midwestern night, not to mention plenty of holiday weekends in the year that follows. But is their relationship reserved for special occasions only...or might there be something much more permanent ahead for them both?

Bram watched Shannon scurry after that assistant of hers—that man with the shrewd eyes and the pesky manners—and he wanted to throttle the guy.

Jake Whatever-The -Hell-His-Last-Name-Was lusted after Shannon—that much was clear. Shannon's feelings toward the assistant were more difficult to ascertain, but Bram would figure it out. He always did.

Why? Because she'd caught his interest. Even if anything beyond tonight was an exercise in futility.

He marched around the perimeter of the dance floor, trying to imagine his ex-girlfriend at a weekend affair like this. Angie would've wanted to hit every activity. Not miss a single second of excitement, whatever the latest thrill might be. She absolutely exhausted him when they were together, but not because he couldn't handle the events she threw his way.

No. He could handle anything.

But her insatiable need for diversion drained him. It felt like a reflection on him. Made him fear his inability to keep her entertained. And he'd hated that.

Pretty-faced women dotted the dance floor. Several looked at him with those eyes filled with feverish anticipation, an expectation that a love match might be imminent. Well, Bram knew better. Relationships were fine as long as they were kept in their proper place. Something hot. Something short-term. Something with boundaries. Try to make them your top priority and everything else in your life would get shot to hell.

He shuddered, flooded by a need to get away from the hopeful expressions etched on the faces of those single women.

So he strode out into the hallway and lingered by a display cabinet featuring, among other things, a curvy stained-glass vase. It was European. Mid-Twentieth Century. Delicate yet intricate. Colorful but in a tasteful, not discordant style.

Funny. In an odd way it reminded him of Shannon.

Now there was a woman whose company he'd admit to enjoying. But, let's face it, she wasn't exactly available to him. If he were being honest with himself—and he'd made a habit out of doing just that—perhaps this was part of his fascination.

She was lovely, but she wouldn't be capable of making demands on him during his hectic workweek. She represented everything that spelled relaxation in his book: Home and hearth, an out-of-the-way locale, feminine cozy comfort nestled in a charming, rustic environment. She was smart, responsible and in full charge of her own career path.

He could almost convince himself his attraction to her was "wholesome." Almost…because he still loved the allure of her most curvaceous assets. And, after a mere twenty seconds of remembering her in his arms as they danced, he knew their potential physical chemistry played no small part in her appeal.

He stared at the vase again, mesmerized by the swirl of colors whenever a stained-glass chip reflected the light. He squinted at it, and the magnificent rainbow was no longer distinct. The hues bled together like silken watercolors, as if, by a mere change in perspective, all the disparate elements of life could join together as one.

"Well, hello again, Bram."

Shannon. Her voice made him open his eyes fully and drink in the vision of her standing before him.

"Crisis averted?" he asked her.

She smiled. "For the time being." She pointed to the display cabinet. "See anything that intrigues you."

He looked right at her. "Yes." He stared into her blue eyes until she blushed. After another moment he added, "And the vase is nice, too."

"Um...well, that's one of my favorites also. My parents took a trip to New York about ten years ago, and they found it in an Old World antique shop there."

"It's pretty," he said, reaching for her hand and entwining her fingers with his. "But I think it belongs elsewhere. In a private home. Atop a fireplace, maybe. It seems too personal for a hallway, even in an inn this cozy."

She let him continue to hold her hand and even took a step closer to him, but her gaze was focused on the vase. Or maybe on something—a memory—further away. "I guess I'd never thought of that way, particularly since I grew up living here at Holiday Quinn. The entire inn was our house, but, I'll admit, it was never especially private."

Bram brought her soft hand toward his face, looked at her for a long moment and then pressed his lips against that smooth skin.

"So, what does a man have to do to get some privacy in this place?"

A flash of passion ignited within her at these words. He could sense it, feel it burning just beneath the surface.

What did he want to have happen here?

A night with her? Yes.

A part of tomorrow? Maybe, maybe not. Goodbyes were difficult…and indefinite. But he'd take his chances on their flame blazing steadily until the morning.

"Bram." His name rolled off her lips in a whisper. He could feel her interest. Her questions. Her deliberation. But he sensed, despite whatever internal battles she waged, she was as curiously enchanted as he.

"Shannon!" Jake called.

And the spell was broken.

Jake jogged up to them. "Excuse me, Shannon, I *hate* to interrupt," he said with frozen, insincere syllables, "but we have another problem."

Shannon sighed and pulled her hand away. Bram's fingers felt the chill of her departure.

"I'm so sorry, Mr. Hartwick," she said with a formality that would have offended him if he hadn't noticed the flicker of disappointment in her eyes. "I'm afraid I have additional business to attend to tonight."

"Perhaps we'll be able to continue our conversation another time," he found himself saying, though he had no immediate plans to return to the inn.

"Perhaps," she replied. Then added, "I hope so."

ABOUT THE AUTHOR

Marilyn Brant is the award-winning women's fiction author of ACCORDING TO JANE (2009), FRIDAY MORNINGS AT NINE (2010) and A SUMMER IN EUROPE (2011), all from Kensington Books. She's also a #1 Kindle Bestseller and writes fun, flirty romantic comedies. Her novels ON ANY GIVEN SUNDAE (2011) and PRIDE, PREJUDICE AND THE PERFECT MATCH (2013) were both Kindle Top 100 Bestsellers in Humor. HOLIDAY MAN (2012) earned numerous 5-star reader reviews online, and DOUBLE DIPPING (2011) was a finalist for Best Contemporary Novel in the 2012 International Digital Awards.

As a former teacher, library staff member, freelance magazine writer and national book reviewer, Marilyn has spent much of her life lost in literature. Her debut novel, ACCORDING TO JANE, featuring the ghost of Jane Austen giving a young woman dating advice, won the Romance Writers of America's prestigious Golden Heart Award and was selected as one of the Top 100 Romance Novels of All Time by Buzzle.com. Her second novel, FRIDAY MORNINGS AT NINE, was a Book-of-the-Month Club and Doubleday pick. And A SUMMER IN EUROPE was featured in the Literary Guild and BOMC2, and it became a Top 20 Bestseller in Fiction & Literature for the Rhapsody Book Club. The Polish translation edition will be coming out in Summer 2013.

She lives in Chicago with her family and is at work on her next novel. Visit her at www.marilynbrant.com.

CPSIA information can be obtained at www.ICGtesting.com
Printed in the USA
LVOW06s1931020114

367801LV00001B/125/P